THE FIVE BARRED GATE

The Five Barred Gate
Copyright © 2019
Jeff S. Bray

Library of Congress Control Number:2019948890
ISBN: 978-1-948679-67-1

Cover concept & design by David Warren

Published by WordCrafts Press
Cody, Wyoming 82414
www.wordcrafts.net

THE FIVE BARRED GATE

a novel of suspense

JEFF S. BRAY

WordCrafts Press

DEDICATION

To those who accept the challenges set before them daily.
May God bless you richly.

J acob was awakened by the sound of his cell door slamming shut. He lifted his swollen, pounding head and looked around. The small opening in the door cast a beam that illuminated a tin bowl and cup. *Dinner is served*, he thought. *Now if I only had an appetite.* Through the pain, he lifted himself off the cold floor and shuffled to the cup. He assumed it to be water. He hoped it was water. He gulped it down.

"Drink sparingly."

Startled, Jacob sloshed water over the rim of the cup.

"Who's there?"

The voice returned.

"No telling when another will come. Eat up though. Some days you only eat once."

"Thanks," Jacob replied and immediately regretted it. Even speaking hurt.

"Are you alright, brother?" the voice sounded genuinely concerned.

"Just peachy. Who *are* you?"

"Where are my manners?" the voice chuckled. "I'm Eric Lassiter." The voice seemed to be coming from a small barred window at the top of the wall.

"I'm Andrews," Jacob replied toward the opening. "Jacob Andrews." He ran his tongue over his split lip and winced. He reached for the bowl, lifted it to his mouth, then paused and gave it a short sniff. He put the bowl back on the floor, its contents unconsumed. "How can you eat this stuff?"

"You get used to it. How are you feeling?"

"I've had better days. How long was I out?"

"About a day." Eric sounded unsure. "I think. It's hard to tell sometimes."

"Yeah, I guess it would be too much to ask for them to put a clock in here." Jacob rested his head against the wall. Its coolness gave his headache some relief. He looked over the room. There was a cot against one wall, furnished with a lone pillow without a pillowcase, and a threadbare blanket that looked like it hadn't been laundered in, well, ever. A steel commode sat in the corner with a roll of paper hanging on the flush handle. *Probably single-ply*, Jacob mused wryly. *These guys think of everything.* The solitary door was fitted with a small open window, secured with four vertical steel bars and on horizontal crossbar. It was enough to allow a modicum of dull light to enter the room, but also enough to prevent anyone from even thinking about wriggling through to freedom.

He wondered if the light was daylight or artificial light. He had no way of knowing.

"I wonder what time it is?" he said aloud.

"Lunch was just served. So, it must be around one o'clock."

Jacob startled. He hadn't expected a response from the guy in the next cell. But he figured any conversation was better than sitting alone with his thoughts.

"Hmm. Considering the angle of the shadows, I would have figured it closer to dinner," Jacob replied.

"I don't think the light is daylight," Eric said. "I've marked the pattern from day to day, and it varies. I think it's just one more way they are trying to mess with our minds. You end up having to take their word for everything."

"You've figured all that out? You must have been here for a while." Jacob asked.

"Eight months—so far."

"Eight months. That sucks. How much longer do you have?"

"I was sentenced to a year," Eric said, his voice flat. "How 'bout you? How long will I have the pleasure of your company?"

"Well, assuming I've been here unconscious for one whole day, so that leaves two months and 29 days." Jacob said. He pulled the spoon from his bowl and dragged the handle against the cell wall. One short line. *Day one.*

"Three months. Is that all? The Official who arrested you must've liked you," Eric chuckled.

"Edwards? Yeah, I'm sure he's adding me to his Christmas card list as we speak." Jacob touched his swollen cheek with his fingers, picking at the crusted, dried blood that had leaked from his scalp. He closed his eyes and leaned back against the cool wall again. The pounding in his head had receded a bit, and he started to drift off.

"So, what happened?"

Eric's sudden interrogation startled Jacob from his drowse.

"Do you always talk so much?"

"No." There was a pause, then a chuckle. "Yes. Yes, I guess I do. I apologize."

Jacob nodded, then his head started throbbing again and he immediately regretted it. "Short version: I was trying to visit my son. His mother wouldn't let me see him. She called the police, but an Official showed up. He got in my face; I got back in his. Next thing I know I'm being tazed and put in cuffs."

"Yeah, that will do it. You do know they monitor police bands, right? If an Official is close enough, they often take it upon themselves to respond to a call."

"Really? No, I didn't know that. Son of a— Well, it all makes sense now. He was there awful quick."

Jacob's memory of his encounter with Official Edwards came flooding back with a vengeance.

"You have no standing here. This is a local matter. Leave us alone!" Jacob shouted at the Official who was standing just inches away.

The Official took exception, "I have the right to intervene where I see fit. Now you need to step back before something bad happens, citizen."

Jacob didn't move. He dug in further and jabbed his finger toward the Officials face, "You're the one who needs to step back. Nobody is going to keep me from seeing my son."

"Sir, I suggest you calm down. You're about two seconds away from me hauling you out of here in handcuffs." The Official was calm. If there was one thing Officials were known for, it was their composure. It was part of their training. 'Maintain your civility, and you remain above reproach,' was one of their core teachings. 'Let the other person escalate the situation, and your actions are justified.' Officials were always calm and civil while in the public eye. Behind closed doors—that was another story.

"I'm not afraid of you," Jacob taunted, "That badge means nothing. You didn't earn it; it was handed to you. You're a glorified hall monitor."

The Official smiled. His demeanor never changed. But the intensity in his voice indicated the severity of his intentions. "That's it!" He grabbed Jacob by the neck and before the hapless citizen could take a breath, he was on the ground with a knee in his back. His arms were wrenched behind him and he felt the steel cuffs engage around his wrists with a sharp click. "By the authority given me by the Governor of the state of Texas, I am placing you under arrest for violation of article JSI2399 of the Federal Speech Act."

Jacob squirmed all the way to the car. "Where are you taking me? You have no right to do this!" He stomped his heel onto the Official's foot and broke free. He started to run, but didn't take more than a few steps before something hit him in the back. A charge pulsed through his body. Everything went black.

Jacob shivered as the memory faded. He shook his head in a vain attempt to dislodge the recollection from his mind, and was rewarded with a return of the incessant pounding in his head. *Note to self: Stop doing that!* "So, friend, what did you do to get here?"

"Short version or long version?"

"Doesn't look like I'm going anywhere anytime soon," Jacob replied. "Long version."

An eerie silence settled over Jacob's cell, broken only by the sound of his breathing. He grew impatient. "You gonna tell me or not?"

More silence.

"Come on, man. A minute ago you were talking up a storm. What's up with that?"

Silence.

"Short version?" Jacob said, "How 'bout you start with the short version?"

"Short version," Eric responds. He blows out a deep breath. "I said the wrong thing, at the wrong time, in the wrong place. Word got back to Official Edwards. I was arrested. Just like you."

"Edwards. Jerk." Jacob spit the name as if it tasted bad.

Silence settled over the cell again. Jacob's mind wandered again to his arrest.

When Jacob regained consciousness he was sitting in a chair with his hands cuffed behind his back, his muscles still contracting from the Taser strike. A cigar smoldered in an ashtray on a table that supported a lamp with a shade. The smoke danced a lazy pirouette within the light, then drifted into the darkness above. Jacob jumped at the sound of a throat being cleared. A man stepped from a dark corner and into the light. It was the Official who had arrested him.

"Good afternoon, sunshine," the Official said. "I wondered how long it would take you to wake up. I am Official Nathan Edwards, and you, my friend, are in a great deal of trouble."

"Was it the glorified hall monitor comment, or my heel to your foot that has put you in such a foul mood?" Jacob sneered.

The Official pulled the baton from his belt and casually swung it, connecting with Jacob's cheek bone, just below his left eye.

The force of the blow rocked Jacob to the side, almost knocking him out of the chair. He could feel the heat of blood rolling down his cheek. He glared at the Official—at both of the Officials, or was it the same Official two times?

The Official laid his baton on the table, sat, picked up his cigar, and took a deep drag. He blew out a perfect smoke ring, then smiled and fixed Jacob with a cold smile. "By all means, Citizen, keep talking. I can do this all day."

"With your weight, I'm amazed you could do anything for an hour, much less a day," Jacob jeered to the Official Edwards on the left.

The smile never left Official Edwards' face, but it never touched his eyes either. He sighed like a kindergarten teacher dealing with a petulant five-year-old. "I can see we're going to have to do this the hard way." He rested his cigar in the ashtray, then called out, "Turner. Anderson. Get in here!"

Two men, or was it four, dressed in tan slacks and black short-sleeved, button-up shirts entered. They're uniforms were identical to Official Edwards, except his shirt was white.

A stray though shot through Jacob's mind. 'They probably wear short sleeves to highlight their muscles. These two sure have a lot to highlight.'

"Yes, sir?"

Official Edwards retrieved cigar and used it to point at Jacob. "This citizen needs a lesson in manners. Will you take him somewhere quiet so he can contemplate his shortcomings? And feel free to assist him in his education."

"Yes, sir!"

With one man on each side, they pulled Jacob to his feet. Official Edwards stood and looked Jacob full in the face. For the first time, the smile left his face.

"Thirty days," he said. "You're lucky I'm in a good mood, citizen. An outburst like that could have easily gotten you a year. Remember that next time."

"Oh, there will be a next time," Jacob declared.

The smile returned to Officer Edwards' lips. "Two months."

"You can't do that, you piece of—"

"I am an Official of the state of Texas. I can do anything," Edwards cut him off. "Three months. Would you care to try for more?"

Jacob bit the inside of his mouth to keep from spewing more venom.

"I thought not. Get him out of here," Edwards commanded.

The two heavily muscled men escorted Jacob down a dark hall to an even darker room. Once inside, they locked the door. Jacob was still cuffed behind his back when they began taking turns punching him with closed fists. They tossed him around the room like a rag doll, only to pick him up and continue their barrage. There was no animosity in their routine; they were just doing their job. And they were very good at their job. From his face to his knees, they left no spot untouched. He was close to losing consciousness when the beating stopped. The next thing he remembered was waking up in his cell.

"Edwards will pay," Jacob declared, his emotions overflowing through his words.

"Careful, the walls have ears," Eric warned.

"Oh, he's the big, bad wolf when you're handcuffed," Jacob ignored the warning. "I'd like to see how he does in a fair fight."

"Kenneth saw how he did in a fair fight," Eric replied.

"Who's Kenneth?"

"Kenneth was the guy who used to occupy your cell. He was a hothead too."

"I am not a hothead!"

"My mistake. I'm sorry. I should have said, he believed in speaking his mind, the same way you do."

"If something needs to be said, I say it!"

"Right."

Silence pervaded the cell. After a few moments, Jacob could stand it no longer.

"Okay, so tell me about Kenneth already."

Eric started his story again. "Like you, Kenneth tended to speak his mind. He said he was going to make Edwards pay when he got out. As I said, the walls have ears. The next day, Edwards showed up in Kenneth's cell. He noted that making threats against state Officials was a capital crime. He politely offered Kenneth the opportunity to retract his threat. Kenneth said he meant every word. Edwards bashed the life out of him, literally. I heard his skull crack against the wall. Two days he laid there, moaning. He died in the cell where you are now confined. I could hear him whimpering. I still do. I'm sure he was unconscious. I hope he was unconscious. Still, that's no way for a man to die."

Jacob sat against the wall in stunned silence. He caressed his swollen cheek, "Did you know him well? Kenneth, I mean?"

"No," Eric whispers.

"How long had he been here?

"Three days," Eric answered. "Please, friend. Remember that next time you think of something that *needs saying*. I've seen enough pain in this place to last a lifetime, and I don't want to add you to the list." After a long pause, Eric added, "And Jacob—Kenneth was not handcuffed when Edwards went after him."

Jacob sat silent, allowing this new information to sink in. He heard whispering coming from Eric's cell. He couldn't make out the words, but it sounded like a prayer. He picked up the bowl of slop and methodically shoveled the food into his mouth, hoping it would ease his stomach pains.

Jacob's thoughts turned to his son. *Barely three and yet so grown. He has no idea what is going on now. Maybe it is for the best.* He thought of Renae—her smile, her frown; how she looked right before she called the police on him. His thoughts turned dark. *I'm on my own. No one is coming to rescue me. Parents dead, no siblings, Renae was all the family I had and I blew it with her. She hates me. And who is this Eric guy, talking to me as if we were long lost friends? Hope I don't end up like Kenneth, bleeding to death on a cold cement floor. I wonder…*

His questions would have to wait. He could hear soft snoring sounds coming from the adjacent cell. He sipped the last of his water, stumbled to his cot, and collapsed onto it. A dripping faucet lulled his pain-wracked body to sleep.

||

Jacob finished his bowl of gruel, as he came to call it. It came late, and just as Eric had said, *sometimes you only eat once*. He had only eaten once today. His previous meal was the morning before. And that bowl wasn't even half full. *If you're hungry enough, even smoothie stew is a welcome sight*, he mused as he slurped down the last spoonful.

"Ah. Good stuff," Eric said from the other side of the wall.

"Keep telling yourself that," Jacob laughed. "Nearly a week, and I still haven't gotten used to it, but it's sustenance, so it will have to do."

He carried his spoon to the wall where he had been drawing his lines. Today he scratched a hash mark across the four horizontal lines that were already there. *Five days. Only 85 more to go.*

Jacob took a step back and examined his handiwork. The marks seemed somehow familiar. Then it clicked. *The five-barred gate. Ms Reimer's second-grade math class.*

Ms Reimer used the method to teach the class to count by fives.

"It helps when you are trying to keep track of a large number of things," Jacob recalled her saying. "Use a line side-by-side to represent one, two, three, and four. Then to complete the group, draw a diagonal line across the four lines. This represents five. Then you can count by fives. It makes it much easier than counting by ones."

She had called the hash marked grouping a "Five-Barred Gate."

Ms Reimer liked using imagery in her teaching. She told the class about the wooden gate on her father's ranch: Four pieces of wood connected diagonally by a long 2x4 that connected them—a five-barred gate. Since then, every time Jacob drove past a ranch with a wooden gate, he would see the number five. Even at 28.

Jacob was jarred from his memories by Eric's repeated question.

"Sorry, what?" Jacob asked.

"I asked you if your headache was any better."

"Oh, that." Jacob rolled his eyes in a circle. They still felt like rubber bands stretched too thin. "Better, but not completely healed," he answered.

Over the last few days, Jacob had gotten to know his neighbor. Or perhaps Eric was getting to know him. They talked about Jacob at great length. His job, or series of jobs over the recent months, from his trucking days to his work as a ranch hand, which led in a roundabout way, to meeting Renae.

"Renae's parents owned the ranch next to Mr. Ingles, the guy I worked for," Jacob explained. "I'd see her drive past when I was tilling a field or repairing a fence work. She was always kicking up dust, and I always tipped my hat and smiled."

"You tipped your hat?" Eric sounded incredulous.

"It's the gentlemanly thing to do," Jacob grinned at the memory, then related how he met his future wife.

"I had gone into town to pick up a bale of barbed wire for Mr. Ingles," he recalled. "Renae was there with her father. I didn't recognize her at first, because she wasn't wearing a pair of large round sunglasses, and she wasn't driving past me at 30 miles per hour. But I knew her father, and when he called her name, that's when I saw them—those large, round sunglasses were perched up on top of her head.

"Well, I tipped my hat and said, 'Afternoon, ma'am.' She just nodded as if I were beneath her notice. Then the shopkeeper said, 'Jacob, we have a bit of a dilemma here. Seems we only have one bale of barbed wire left, and Renae here placed an order for a bale last week.'

"'I suppose that means this bale, is our bale,' she said sweetly, smiling at me as if she had won the lottery. I said, 'Yes, ma'am, I suppose it does, but you see, I was supposed to order that bale two weeks ago, and if Mr. Ingles sees me coming back to the ranch without it, well, I could lose my job. And you wouldn't want that to happen, now would you?'

"Renae got this oh-so-concerned look on her face and said, 'I'm so sorry, Mr.—' she trailed off, just waiting for me to say my name. I let her hang a second or two then said 'Jacob.' I laughed when she called me 'Mr. Jacob.' I made the correction and her voice dropped all low and embarrassed. 'Oh, Jacob. Mr. Ingles hired hand?' she said. And I answered, 'Yes ma'am.' Then her eyes lit up in recognition, 'I see you sometimes when I'm driving down the road to my parents' home.'

"I liked that she remembered me. So, I showed her that I remembered her too, 'You drive a Green Civic. I see you too—well, what's left of you after that cloud of dust settles.' Then I asked her to find it in her heart to me with the fix I was in.

"She just gave me a pitiful kind of pout and said, 'I'm sorry Jacob, but there is only one. Since we ordered it and you didn't, it's only fair that we get it.' She said it sweetly enough, but there was no mistaking her meaning. I had lost. I said, 'Very well, darlin'. But if you see me by the side of the road with a 'Will Work for Food' sign you better stop and help me out.'

Jacob paused for a drink of tepid water, and Eric asked, "What did she say to that?"

Jacob gave a low chuckle. "She said, 'Don't call me darlin'. My name is Renae.' Two weeks later, I had a date. And I kept my job. Renae's dad called Mr. Ingles and told him that he was grateful that his polite hired hand generously gave up his bale of barbed wire. He told Mr. Ingles he was the one who forgot to order it, and that I had saved him a nagging from his old lady."

Jacob grew solemn at the memory, then continued. "Renae and I dated for a few months, then I proposed. We were married six months later. Michael was born the following year."

"Not one for waiting, huh," Eric said.

"When you know, you know," Jacob agreed. "Besides, life is too short for waiting. You never know how much time you have left."

There was silence for a while.

"Okay Eric, enough about me. It's your turn. Spill it."

"I am a pastor," Eric said, his voice low and warm. "At lease, I used to be one."

"Preacher, huh? From all the questions I assumed you were a bartender or a taxi driver." Jacob paused; the thought tasted rancid in his mouth. "Or a plant. Sorry."

Eric laughed. "It's alright. I wondered the same about you."

"So, did you have a church?"

"Yes," Eric said. "Yes, I did. Our Savior's Cross Baptist Church. It is, or was, over in Polk. It's been closed for a while now. It was taken away from me, and I was put in here, over a sermon I preached."

"Must have been one hell of a sermon," Jacob jested.

"Yes, I suppose it was," Eric chuckled. "We were forced to shut our doors after I said something considered illegal in one of my sermons, thanks to the Speech Act. Edwards had planted someone within my congregation to monitor my behavior. You know, to make sure I stayed politically correct."

Jacob nods his head in understanding. "Yeah, the good ol' Speech Act. I know it all too well."

"What was intended to silence political protesters and rabble-rousers, was stretched and re-interpreted to encompass the whole Anti-Dehumanization Act that was passed two years before."

"The Anti-Dehumanization Act?" Jacob pondered for a moment as a memory tickled his brain. "Didn't that come from the case where that guy in Atlanta tried to sue that church? What two, three years ago?"

"Four years. But yes, that's the one," Eric said. "Someone in the church didn't like it when the pastor preached about everyone having sinned and fallen short of the glory of God. He was offended to be called 'sinner' along with everyone else. In short, he sued. He didn't win the Federal case because there was no precedent set in Federal law. But he filed and won a civil suit against the preacher, the church, and the denomination for $2.1 million for dehumanization."

"Insane. How did things escalate so fast?" Jacob asked.

"The District Attorney on that case lobbied to get precedent in Georgia. Georgia was the first state where it became illegal to publicly offend someone. The Federal government liked the idea. First the president issued an Executive Order, then congress passed it into law. Some happily assimilated the new law. Others filed suit and tried to have it overturned. Texas was one of them.

"The Texas government wanted to curb the movement and have the laws thrown out. But the Justice Department started the Federal Peace Board which appointed federal peace officers, commonly referred to as Officials. They're like federal marshals with jurisdiction across the nation. Official Edwards was appointed to the South Texas Jurisdiction with authority to hire deputies. Two of them I'm sure you've met."

"Yes, I have," Jacob said, caressing his bruised ribs. "Crazy what our country has come to when you can't even legally state your own opinion."

"I know. Makes you think though, before you speak, I mean."

"Not even five years ago, you could tell someone they were fat and ugly. Then a guy might get mad and try to punch you in the face, but now saying that can land you in jail? Unbelievable. I mean, I'm not so blunt to call someone names, but yeah, I say things to people to get their attention. I guess it could be considered a little insulting, but I say it to help the person to change, to better themselves. Now people get offended and lash out, saying their 'rights' are being violated. I just don't get it. When did everyone become so soft?"

"It's the times we live in, Jacob. It's easier to be offended and complain than to want to make a change. It's too hard for people to see there are different points of view."

"Well, people need to toughen up. All of this *hurt feelings* garbage makes me sick."

Silence settled over the two men for a moment.

"Tell me more about your infamous sermon," Jacob said.

"Not much more to tell, really," Eric said. "I was preaching about repentance. "The central theme was, 'Only God can save. Nothing or no one else can save, not even the government.' Criticizing the government is illegal. I knew that. And I wasn't actually trying to be critical, but God called me to preach the truth. The government can do a lot of things—good things, like providing social services and health care and such—but it can't save your soul. Word of my 'disloyal and seditious' sermon was reported to Official Edwards, and here I am."

"You must have known your sermon could be misinterpreted and get you into trouble with the law. Why say it in public like that?"

"I would be in greater danger if I didn't preach the gospel the way God leads me to. Like the old saying, 'Better to die on my feet before God, than on my knees before man.' Besides, what greater death could one ask for?"

"Who said anything about dying? You got a year in prison. Bad enough, but they're not hanging people—yet. Sounds pretty scary, though. Guess you take your God thing seriously?"

"I do," Eric murmured. "I do. Plus I didn't think I would get caught."

They both laughed.

"Do you know what Kenneth was in for?"

"I haven't a clue."

"So, you didn't speak to him?"

"No, no, not really. Kenneth was full of hate and anger. I tried to talk with him once, but he cussed me out, and told me to shut the… well, you get the picture. I respected his wishes."

"And now he's gone."

"Yes. Now he's gone."

The thought of Kenneth dying in his cell sent a chill down

Jacob's spine. *Maybe Kenneth's angry spirit is still trapped in this cell with me, sending bad juju. I think Eric feels it too. I can hear it in his voice.*

Jacob shook the thought from his brain. "Why does time go so slowly here?"

"Slowly? Why I haven't noticed." Eric quipped.

"Oh, sorry," Jacob said, genuinely abashed. "I forgot. Gosh, it really must seem like an eternity to you. Eight months. And I'm whining after five days. You must be going crazy by now."

Jacob could hear Eric getting comfortable. He put his bowl back by the door and laid down as well. *Eric's right; you can't tell day from night in this place. If not for my marks on the wall I wouldn't know if this was day 12 or day three. Day three. Kenneth died on day three. Great. Back to Kenneth again.* Jacob let out another echoing sigh and drifted off to sleep with a man he had never met speaking unspoken words to his mind.

|||

Jacob startles awake. It is still night, so his internal clock says. His cell door is wide open. He rises from his bunk and slowly walks over to it.

"Eric?"

Eric doesn't answer. He calls two more times. Still no response. He peeks his head out of his cell, half expecting a baton to come down on his head and hear Edwards squealing, *'That's what you get for peeking out, citizen.'* But nothing happened.

A line of cell doors line the dark hallway. They are all closed. The sound of a dripping faucet echoes from the end of the corridor. *Last cell maybe?* Taking a chance, Jacob edges out of his cell and takes a few tentative steps. He stops in front of Eric's cell and calls out again.

"Eric?"

No response.

There is a solid door at the end of the hall; it is different than the others. Jacob tiptoes toward it. The floor is cold under his bare feet. He can feel the smooth linoleum finish, unlike the coarse cement of his cell. His heart is a bass drum between his ears, rhythmically throbbing louder the closer he approaches. As he reaches for the handle, he hears a pained moan from the other side. Once again, he whispers for Eric. As before, no reply.

The handle makes a loud *click*, and the steel door creaks as it turns on its hinges, ending any chance of secrecy. He glances over his shoulder—*no one there*—he presses on. It is darker in this room. *The drip is definitely coming from in here. The corner maybe?*

The light from the hallway casts a dim ray toward the back wall. Jacob sees a figure prostrate on the ground. He crosses to the body and kneels beside it. Assuming the worst, he places his hand on the figure's back. His fear is confirmed, no breathing. *Whoever he is, he's dead.* Jacob turns the body over, then leaps to his feet screaming. *It's Kenneth.* A switch is flipped and the overhead bulb bathes the room in a harsh glaring light. A gravelly voice demands, "What are you doing in here?!"

Jacob leapt from his cot, sweaty and heart pounding. He was still in his cell; he never left. But he was still screaming.

"Another dream?" Eric asked.

"Yes."

"That's three this week."

"Yeah." Jacob sat back on his cot and placed his head between his hands, elbows on knees, trying to will his breathing back to normal.

"I just can't..."

"Kenneth again?" Eric inquired.

Jacob nodded, then laughed to himself. Eric couldn't see him. His nod was useless. "How do I even know it's him? I've never even seen the guy. But it's the same dream every time, only each time it gets a little bit worse, and it always ends the same; Kenneth dead on a cell floor."

"Could be fear of your unknown future and unrepairable past are wrestling for control of your mind," Eric offered.

It sounded reasonable; a bit overstated, but plausible. Could Kenneth's past be his future? Would his outspoken nature be controlled after he was released? Could it, like Kenneth, lead to his demise? Obviously, that was what landed him here—but how much of that nature still played into who he was now?

"Perhaps you feel a connection with him," Eric continued. "Or more likely, you see how he ended up. You have a realization that your life is headed in that direction. You don't want to go that way, but you don't know where to begin. You want to get your life back, but you're not sure where you jumped the track." Eric paused as a though crossed his mind. "How old are you Jacob?"

"Twenty-eight.

"So, you would still have been in high school when your parents passed?"

"Yes, my junior year," Jacob said, recalling the accident that took their lives. "I was such a mess that year; I almost didn't pass."

"But you did."

"Yeah," Jacob smiled at the small triumph. "I made two decisions that year. One—my senior year was going to be dedicated to them. My focus was going toward graduating head of my class. I would make every effort to make the most of every moment. For them."

"That's honorable. And two?"

"Two? Well, I had so many things left unsaid to them. Both my parents were hard working. They wanted to make sure I had a better life than they did. After my mom had me, there were complications; she almost died. The doctors saved her, but at a cost. She wouldn't be able to have any more children. They gave everything they had for me, their only son.

"They were heading back from Ft Worth when it happened," Jacob recalled. "They were up there getting information on apartments close to the college I would be attending, so we would have time to start saving. On their way back, just outside of Waco, a drunk teen forced them off the road. The car rolled, and they died in the crash.

"They were in Ft. Worth for me," Jacob continued, wiping away tears. "There was so much I wanted to say to them, and I never got the chance, ya know? I made a promise to myself. Since l was unable to thank them for all they had sacrificed for me, I was never going to leave anything unsaid ever again."

"I see," Eric said.

"If it hadn't been for Jesse, my best friend since grade school, I don't think I could have made it. He's the one who got me back on track. He made sure I was in class, helped me with homework, and got me through finals. He was there when I blew out my knee at the beginning of my senior year, and football evaporated from my future. He drove me to school and helped me up the stairs to Algebra II.

"Six months later, we walked across the stage together, graduating in the top 10 percent of our class. Jesse eventually became the first one I gave my first *Missed Opportunity* speech on. He received it well, and it felt good to tell him how much he meant to me. Yeah, I was uncomfortable at first, you know, talking that way, but after a few others, it just became natural. If I had something to say—good, bad—I said it. Just in case I didn't have another opportunity. But, then—"

"Things got out of hand," Jacob and Eric said in unison. They both laughed.

"Right before Renae and I were married, Mr. Ingles passed away. He had been a father-figure to me. He took a chance on me, took me under his wing, gave me purpose. After he died, my MO speeches took on a life of their own, only after losing him there wasn't much good left in them. Things got easier to say, but even when I wanted to convey something positive, the words turned into negativity and condescension. People started avoiding me…"

"Ya think?" Eric interjected.

"I know, right? Jacob nodded in agreement. First my friends, then Renae, then eventually no one would listen when I spoke. It got to the point that even when I said something positive, no one listened. Even Jesse began avoiding me."

"I can understand that. Once you become known for the negative, no amount of positive matter."

"Funny. I made that commitment to not leave anything unsaid to honor my parents. Look where it's gotten me.'" Jacob picked up his spoon and crossed to his makeshift calendar. "I don't think they would be proud of the man I have become. I've failed." He deliberately etched another line—Number 22—then slid down and sat against the wall.

"Every failure is the beginning of a new adventure," Eric replied with a level of authority in his voice Jacob hadn't heard. Even Eric felt empowered by it.

"That's pretty heavy," Jacob says.

"A sermon I preached a couple of years ago. I haven't thought about that in a long time."

It dawned on Jacob that in the three weeks he's been talking to him, Eric had not once mentioned God. No Bible verse-laced admonitions, no judgement, no condemnation. Other than when he prayed before his meal and bed, the guy kept his religion to himself. *Weird. Wasn't he supposed to be a pastor? Isn't poking their nose into other people's business, and forcing their beliefs on the great unwashed supposed to be their thing?*

"So, Eric, why haven't you tried to convert me yet? I mean, I'm kind of a captive audience."

There was no response for an uncomfortable moment. Jacob assumed his prison-mate was pondering some grandiose answer that would split open the heavens and rain down rose petals.

"I'm not sure, Jacob. I suppose I just felt led to refrain from saying anything yet. Too soon, maybe. Perhaps your spirit isn't ready to receive it. It's not that I didn't want to, and I'm certainly not ashamed to. When it comes to the Lord, I'm quite like you. When you feel something needs saying, you say it. When I feel like the Lord needs me to say something, I say it. But unlike you, when God tells me to not say something, I don't say it. In your case, God told me to wait. I've prayed every night for the right time to come. And when that time comes, I'll talk."

Jacob pondered that response for a while. It wasn't the answer he expected. But then, nothing about the guy in the next cell was what he expected for someone in lockup.

"You think your God can help me?" Jacob asked, surprised by his own question.

"I know He can my friend," Eric replied. "He's your God too. Even if you don't know it yet."

"I dunno. I've messed up so many lives—Renae's, Michael's, Jesse's, my in-laws. I can only imagine how many others I've hurt by the things I have said. Not to mention getting myself thrown in here. It's my mess. Why would God want to help me out?"

"Let me tell you a story," Eric said. Jacob could hear a smile in his voice. "There once was a man, much like you, who always had to speak his mind. He was always looking for a fight. He was an informer for the authorities. His job was to wait in the shadows for Christians to talk about Jesus. It was an offensive thing. When they did, he would arrest them. Some were imprisoned; some were executed—men, women… children. He thought he was doing good.

"You can imagine how many lives and families Saul had ruined. Before you object, I know you didn't kill anyone. But negative words can kill the spirit, which is just as hurtful. Saul thought he was doing the right thing; making life better. Then one day while he was on his way to another town in search of more Christians to arrest, a bright light shined down from heaven. And God himself spoke to Saul. As you might imagine, Saul was pretty scared, but God explained that what he was doing is wrong, and that Jesus was in fact who he claimed to be—the Son of God. Then Saul received a whole new mission. Instead of condemning Christians, he was commissioned by God to preach about Jesus. God even gave him a new name—Paul."

"Paul? You mean, like they guy in the Bible?" Jacob asked.

"Yeah, the same guy who wrote quite a bit of the New Testament," Eric answered. "He was also one of the first missionaries, going from town to town, and country to country, telling people what God had done for him. God forgave his past and gave him a future."

"So, Saul goes from killing Christians to making converts? Must have been tough trying to convince people he had really changed," Jacob noted. "I'm not sure I would have trusted the guy."

"No doubt," Eric agreed. "Paul was able to overcome the

doubts of the Christians. But he did make enemies of those who had originally sent him. Those who had originally sent him were now trying to kill him. But God had his hand on him, and he escaped each time."

"He went from the hunter to the hunted."

"Exactly. I'm not gonna lie to you. Paul didn't have it easy. He was shipwrecked, beaten, spent much of the rest of his life in prison. But God was with him through it all. God took someone who was hard-hearted and softened him up. And the words he wrote 2,000 years ago are still affecting people today.

"Jacob, God is that loving. No one has walked so long in the darkness that they can't come to the light. Paul was able to change. You can change too. All it takes is the willingness to change. God sent his son, Jesus, to this world to die for all the sin that you have committed. His death covers all of them—Past, present, and future.

"The best part is that Jesus did not stay in that grave; He rose again. Not only did He conquer sin, but he also conquered death by rising from the dead. That guarantees our future. All we have to do is to accept it. Paul accepted it—he was forgiven. You and I may not get a spotlight from heaven, but we all go through the same change, turning from that old life and living for Jesus."

"That simple? Just accept it?" Jacob asked with disbelief. *Why has no one told me this story before?*

"Crazy, right?"

"Crazy is right! But I don't know." Jacob lowered his head into his hands. "Perhaps when I get myself together. I'm in no condition to come to God right now."

"Jacob, that is the best part. You don't have to have it all together. God accepts you, just as you are. Broken is the perfect condition to be in."

Jacob sat in silence, soaking his friend's words in. He smiled and quipped, "Man, ask one question, and open up the floodgates."

"Yes," Eric chuckled. "Yes, I guess it did. I told you when I feel the urge; I say what I need to say."

Everything was still for a moment. In the quiet a distant dripping made its presence known.

Jacob broke the silence. "I guess it is pointless to ask you what time it is?" Feeling his lack of sleep, he stood and walked to his cot. "I'm going to try and get some sleep—hopefully Kenneth-free."

"Good night, my friend." Eric didn't press any further. The seed was planted. It was up to the Lord on how Jacob would receive it.

Jacob stared at the ceiling, the sleep he craved eluding him. It wasn't nightmares keeping him awake, but Eric's words that were still dancing through the air; Not what he said, but how he said it. He spoke with authority. It had a convinced-beyond-all-doubt sound. *Could Jesus be real?*

IIII

A little more than a week passed without another word about their conversation that night. Jacob laid awake, staring at six five-barred gates etched into his cell wall. One full month of this solitude; two more to go. Even with the voice of his neighbor, he felt alone—alone with his thoughts. *I wonder what Renae is doing right now; where she and Michael are?* He remembered the look on her face as Edwards drove away from what used to be *their* home, before she kicked him out and relegated him to an apartment on the other end of town.

He can still taste his final words to her. And the final words she said to him cut deep. It made him glad that Michael was young. *He won't remember any of this. He won't recall words like 'hate' or 'regret.' He won't recall the yelling or threats. He won't remember 'that time daddy said to mommy.' Thank the Lord for that.* The Lord. The name echoes in Jacob's mind.

"Eric," Jacob whispered. "You awake?"

"Yes, I'm awake. What can I do for you?

Jacob was silent for a moment; not sure what he wanted to ask. He was curious about Paul, but he was even more curious about God. *Paul went to prison for God. Who would be worth doing that for? Who is this Jesus?* He guessed that was the real question.

"Tell me more about Jesus. I mean, I can kinda relate to what Paul went through, but I don't understand how a change in a man's life can be so dramatic based on something he only heard about."

Eric pondered for a moment. "Well, let me begin with Paul. He was an educated man, a scholar. He knew about the prophecies concerning Christ. He was intimately familiar with the Old Testament scriptures. Remember, this was before the New Testament was written. So, when God spoke to him on the road to Damascus, he realized that all he had been taught had come to pass. This Jesus the disciples spoke of was real. He took what he already knew and added his experience with God and preached on that."

"And Jesus?"

"Ahh, Jesus." Eric's voice lit up. "Jesus was God in human form. The short version goes like this: God created all things. God created man. Satan deceived man into sinning. Sin separates man from God. God wanted to be reunited with Man. God implemented a sacrificial system to cover man's sins. But it wasn't enough."

"Sacrifices, like killing bulls and goats to appease the gods, like in Greek mythology?"

"Right, but these sacrifices were instituted by the living God. However, traditional sacrifices were not perfect and needed to be repeated. What was needed was a perfect sacrifice. The only way would be for a man to die; lambs and goats only worked partially. The problem was that man was sinful. Only perfect blood could do the job. So, God sent his son into the world."

"Jesus?"

"Right, Jesus. He was born of a virgin but was human in every way, yet, he was without sin. He began his ministry when he was around 30 years old, and he selected 12 men to follow him closely. Those men were to be witnesses to what happened and to spread the good news."

"Like Paul?" Jacob asked.

"Kind of. Paul came later. But the government didn't like Jesus. So, they arrested, tried, and sentenced Him to be crucified. He died, even though he was innocent—a perfect sacrifice. He was buried on Friday, and early Sunday morning he rose from the grave by the power of God.

"His blood provides forgiveness of sin. It tore away the barrier that was between God and us. Jesus' resurrection gave us power over the consequences of death and allows us to be reunited with him when we die."

Eric finished and allowed silence to settle.

At last Jacob said, "That was the short version?"

Eric laughed. "Yes, yes, it was."

"Sorry," Jacob said. "I tend to blurt. So, Jesus *is* God?"

"Yes, He is," Eric says. "He confined himself to a single form. As God, he is omnipresent, which means he is everywhere. But he humbled himself because of his love for us. He lived on earth for thirty-some-odd years. Felt every emotion we feel, tempted with every sin we are tempted with, lived as a human. And died as a human, because of his love for us."

"Every sin?"

"Every sin. That's the best part. His sacrifice covers all sin. All we have to do is to accept it. It is a free gift. 2 Corinthians 5:17 says, 'Therefore, if anyone is in Christ, he is a new creation; the old has gone, the new has come.' When we believe in him, we are saved. Yes, we will still battle sin, and we still will die, but only our bodies die. Our spirit will live on in Heaven. Only one qualification. When you believe, you need to live for Him. Which means turning your back on your old sinful ways and follow his direction in your life."

"How do I know what that is?"

"Prayer, for one. The Bible is another good source. Get involved with a good church. There is a benefit to being around other believers. Corporate experiences benefit each other. But in here, I would rely on prayer. I have scripture: all the verses I memorized from the time I was a child, through my teens, and on into seminary and my career as a pastor. I can share some of those with you, but I can only give you advice; I can't give you direction. That's different for everyone, and only the Holy Spirit can give you that."

"Thank you," Jacob said.

"You're welcome. Anything else?"

"No, that's all for now." Jacob rolled over in his cot. "I'll let you get some sleep."

"Good night."

"Good night."

Sleep still played hide-and-seek with Jacob's mind. At last he whispered, "God, if you are real and are willing to accept me despite all the crap I've done, then I want to accept that gift. I don't know exactly what that means, other than I want to believe what Eric says about you. Please, show me you are real. Maybe not a bright light, that would be kinda freaky. But in some way show me."

Eric smiled in his cell. Sound carried in this prison. He heard every word. More importantly, he knew that God heard every word too.

A smile crossed Jacob's face as he put down his empty bowl of breakfast gruel. He took his utensil and strolled to his calendar wall. Seventeen bunches of five, plus four. He makes the final slash completing the final five-barred gate—day 90. Tomorrow he will be free. *Three months of near isolation. Three months of these suffocating stone walls. Day after day of monotony, bowls of gruel, which I did get used to, and that ever-persistent drip coming from God knows where—the room down the hall, if those dreams are to be believed.*

The highlight of it all? The friendship he developed with Eric, a man he had gotten to know intimately but has never seen. He'd gained quite a bit of knowledge from their conversations over the past three months. After his prayer, something changed inside him; he couldn't learn enough about Jesus. His hunger grew, and Eric's willingness to feed that hunger created a bond of friendship.

"Almost that time," Eric said through the wall.

"You're right behind me Eric," Jacob replied. "You'll be out before you know it. Then we can get together over a cup of coffee and some real food."

"Jacob, you know it's going to be difficult, right?"

"Yes, I've thought about that. Quite a bit actually," Jacob admitted. "But I'm not sure I care. I mean, I care, but not in a way that would sway me back to who I was a couple of months ago. I've decided I'm going to find Renae and try to make amends. I'm going to apologize for the pain I caused her and Michael. If she accepts it, wonderful, if not, then I'm no worse off than I am now. I don't deserve her forgiveness. I've said some awful things to her that I'm not proud of, but that's all in the past. All I can do is say I'm sorry. Then the ball will be in her court. I just want to see my son."

"That's a good attitude. Just don't forget Paul."

Jacob laid down on his cot, folded his arms across his chest, and stared at the pitted ceiling with a smile. "I can't wait to grab a Bible when I get out of here. I want to read more about Paul. I can really relate to the guy. I'm amazed by what you have remembered over the years."

"I'm glad to hear that," Eric says. "Just be aware that people you think are your friends may not be so quick to believe in this *new* you. They may reject you. So be prepared."

"I have the Lord on my side. If they are meant to accept me, then God will prepare them, just as He prepared Peter for Paul."

Eric smiled at Jacob's recollection of one of his teachings.

"I know it will be a long road. I'll just be grateful when you get released next month."

Jacob laced his fingers behind his head. He connected the ceiling dots to make one of the constellations that he's missed seeing; that he would see this time tomorrow. "I can tell you one thing; it'll be a long time before I ever get past the taste of gruel."

†††

Jacob didn't have much trouble getting to sleep that night; no dreams of Kenneth—those ended weeks ago. He wasn't afraid anymore. A comfort was building up within him. He no longer had a negative outlook. *I've got a handle on it; I can control the things I want to say. Of course, the real test will be on the outside. It's one thing to get comfortable with one person and not fall into old habits; it's quite another to be in public with opinions inundating you.*

Morning came with the rattling of keys and the lock on Jacobs cell clicking. The door opened, and out of the glow of yellow light, someone stepped into his cell. It was Edwards. "Well, well, citizen, it's release day. I hope your time here in my hotel has served as a warning for the next time you chose to open your mouth." Edwards tapped his baton on the edge of the cot making a metallic clanking sound.

"Yes, sir," Jacob says. This time, no fire burned within him, urging him to lash out at the smug expression on the Official's face. "I have learned quite a bit during my stay."

Turner and Anderson waited behind Edwards for his orders. Edwards laughed. "Welcome back into society. You've already met my associates. These gentlemen will…" he paused as if searching for the right words, "*finalize* your paperwork. You should be released by lunch." Laughing, he walked out of the cell and shut and locked the door. His laughter faded into the distance.

"I'm sorry Jacob," Eric said, knowing what was coming.

"It is what it is."

Edwards' deputies arrived, as promised, just before the lunch hour. They did finalize his paperwork, but not before giving him something to remember, courtesy of Official Nathan Edwards. It wasn't the beating he received when he arrived at the facility, but it was enough. Somewhere in the middle of the beating he was given papers to sign. Then it was over. He is a free man. Laying on the floor in a splatter of spit mingled with blood, just before he lost consciousness Jacob heard a clock chime 12. As Edwards promised, Jacob was released by lunchtime.

Jacob opened his eyes, swollen and burning from the salt of his dried sweat. He found himself lying on the couch in his apartment. The clock on the wall showed 2:34 p.m. He had no memory of coming home. *Turner and Anderson must've brought me here.* His body ached, but it was the ache of a free man. He turned his gaze to the ceiling. *No more pitted granite; just the same old white stucco ceiling I been looking at since Renae kicked me out almost a year ago.*

His stomach rumbled. Jacob lifted his beaten body and stood. He was wobbly, but at least he could stand upright. That was something. He walked into the kitchen in search of a meal. Amazingly, the power was still on. He'd paid his six-month lease in advance, so he still had a roof over his head. He did not open the fridge knowing it would contain absolutely nothing of value, but the freezer would be another story. It was always stocked with frozen meals. *A couple of Hungry Mans would hit the spot right about now.*

Jacob ate three frozen dinners and was still hungry. The curse of the gruel was that it was never quite enough. Always being a little hungry was part of Edwards' punishment style. Give you just enough to keep you going, but not enough for you to be satisfied.

As he nuked a fourth meal, his eye caught a picture of him and Michael, stuck on the fridge with a magnet—Jacob in a green hospital gown with matching cap holding his blue-blanketed bundle of joy. The image brought back a flood of memories. He particularly recalled the look of exhausted happiness on Renae's face as their eight-pound rock was handed to her.

After the nurses cleaned Michael up and wrapped him in the blanket, he wanted to take a picture. They admonished him when he went to take a selfie with his son. He remembered saying something mean and took the photo anyway. Looking back, he realized what he said to the nurse was hurtful and uncalled for.

How many others have I hurt?

The timer hit zero and the incessant beeping snapped him out of his daze. He turned off the timer, but left the Hungry Man in the microwave. He returned to the sofa and plopped down, pondering the hurtful things he'd said in his past. "Lord," he prayed aloud, "I know I've hurt so many people, too many to count. While I don't remember all of them, I pray you help me make things right with as many as I can. Help me avoid any chance of hurting anyone again." Feeling a bit cleaner on the inside, Jacob opened his eyes, took a deep breath, and sauntered back into the kitchen to retrieve his fourth meal of the night from "Chef Mike." He ate every bite.

I've still got three more TV dinners, but they're not gonna last, he mused. *Need to go shopping. Well, need to get a job, so I can pay for going shopping.*

Jacob was fired from his last job a couple of weeks before getting arrested, so he had no job to go back to. As Jacob tossed the carcass of his final Hungry Man into the trash, he remembered the coffee can in the pantry. He'd always stashed a couple hundred dollars in it; his rainy day fund, he called it. *Well, it's raining right now.* He grabbed a chair from the dining room and carried it into the kitchen pantry. He stood on it to reach the highest shelf and pulled down a dusty Maxwell House can. Smiling he popped the top and pulled out exactly nothing.

"Son of a— Now what?" Jacob sputtered. He threw the can across the room, gaining little satisfaction from hearing it clatter off the wall and spin to a stop on the floor. He stumbled back to the sofa, feeling more than a little defeated. He started pondering the reality of his new normal.

Car was most likely impounded, he stewed, *or with Official Edwards's demeanor, torched and burned to ashes. The only way to find out is to phone the county impound yard. And that's not gonna happen. I left my cell phone in the car that's in the impound yard. But I would have to walk there, and it's two miles, not sure I'd make it on foot.* Jacob looked at the clock. *It's too late anyway. They'd be closed before I got there. Plus, the coffee can's empty, not that there would have been enough to cover three months' worth of storage fees.*

"Well, this sucks," Jacob said aloud.

Frustrated, Jacob grabbed the remote and turned on the television.

"To reactivate service, please call your provider" scrolled across the screen.

With a sigh, Jacob shut the TV off and tossed the remote onto the coffee table. Unbidden memories start playing tag in his brain. He thought of Renae and the night that put the final nail in the coffin of their relationship. He had been let go from the job where he worked at for almost six months. *Downsizing* they said. *Business flow no longer warranted having so many drivers* they said. Instead of cutting loads, they cut him—and he didn't take it well. He'd worked hard this time. It was the longest he had held a job since he worked with Mr. Ingles. He was a new father. He hadn't done anything wrong, for crying out loud.

The entire way home, he rehearsed how he was going to deliver the bad news to Renae. But his thoughts turned toward his boss, and he started reliving their conversation when he was let go. All the things he should have said roiled in his mind and turned his stomach to acid. By the time he pulled into his driveway and turned off the car he was furious. Every inch of frustration he felt for his former boss, he direct at Renae.

"You're home early." Renae was folding laundry.

"Yes," Jacob said, tossing the keys onto the counter.

Renae let out a sigh. She knew the signs all too well. "What happened this time, Jacob?"

"I don't know. Bossman is an idiot." Jacob's go-to excuse for losing a job. He opened the fridge, grabbed a soda and sat down at the kitchen table.

"You said something to him, didn't you?"

"Well Darlin', if something needs to be said, I—" he said, even though this time he hadn't. It was his usual response to her baiting him. It usually made her laugh.

"Stop it. That used to be cute, now it's just annoying. It sounds so condescending, and I don't like it."

"I'm not condescending. You always take it that way. And your attitude is not helping. You're never on my side. Aren't you supposed to be my wife?"

"Jacob, I…" She shut the dryer door and left the room.

Jacob heard the bedroom door slam. Then he heard her start to cry.

That was it. She'd had enough. One to many "You always" and "You never." That night Renae packed a suitcase for her and Michael, and they went to her parents. By the end of the week, they had decided it would be best for him to move out. Reluctantly, he did.

He would later find out that she had become emotionally distraught over his verbal abuse. He had never laid a hand on her, but his words stung. He knew that now. Words echo in your mind at night after everyone else is asleep. Words imprint themselves on your subconscious until you either believe them, or you reject them and push away the one saying them.

How many others have I hurt?

Jacob didn't like the man he had been. For so long his tongue was a weapon. Lashing out. He felt like he was only doing his duty. *I suppose this is how Paul felt after he came to the light.* The pain of realization. The guilt of hurting so many doing what he thought was the right thing. Paul surely knew that pain. Jacob certainly felt it.

Jacob wished he had a Bible. Then he snapped his fingers. *Renae's Bible!* He remembered that she had stowed it away in one of the boxes he left with. A fact that, at the time he discovered it, he was not happy about at all.

He went to the closet and stared rummaging through what he had hastily packed. He found the box and opened it. There it was, Renae's Bible. It smelled like her. Jacob remembered the lotion she would put on before bed, right before she pulled it out to *"read until she felt sleepy."*

Jacob couldn't remember ever opening a Bible, at least not intentionally. He never berated Renae for reading it. It just didn't matter to him. He never gave it a second thought.

Now he wished he could go back and read it with her. Things might have been different.

It wasn't that Renae went to church much, She didn't. But she always kept her Bible in the drawer of her nightstand and read it regularly. Until Michael was born. After that she didn't have much time for reading, or anything else. She was *a little preoccupied*, she would say. Between feedings and cleanings, she was busy and exhausted. *And a little overprotective*, Jacob thought.

"Does he feel warm to you?" was one of Renae's favorite questions.

"Yes, honey, but you have him wrapped up in two blankets and it's 80 degrees. I'd be warm too." Jacob would respond.

That would make her laugh.

Jacob carried the precious book to the couch, sat, and opened to the book of Acts. He searched for the first mention of Paul. He had heard Eric's version of the story. He wanted to read it for himself, firsthand. And there it was. Paul was still Saul. He was on a crusade to imprison those who were called Christians. He read about the encounter on the road to Damascus: the blinding light, the voice from heaven, the blindness, the meeting with Ananias, and the restoration of his sight. It was all just as Eric had said.

Jacob read of Paul proclaiming Jesus as the Messiah, the conspiracy to kill him, and his escape; about Paul ending up in Jerusalem with the disciples who feared him and only Barnabas standing up for him, proclaiming that his conversion was the real deal. Jacob marvels at the destroyer of the church being chosen to take the gospel to the Gentiles.

Maybe Eric can be my Barnabas, to convince others my conversion is real?

Jacob devoured the story of Paul and Barnabas traveling together, followed by Paul traveled with Silas, the companions being in prison together, then separated. Of Paul remaining in prison, having meetings with official after official, eventually being sent to Caesar, then on his way enduring shipwreck for three months, and eventually making his way to Rome.

Before Jacob knew it, he was deep into the book of Romans. Questions flood him about Jesus. He backtracked to Matthew and started reading the gospels. When he paused to look at the clock he was startled to realized it was 3:45 a.m. His eyes were heavy, so he made his way to the bedroom. With a smile, he laid down experiencing a peace he hadn't known since long before his parents died.

Much more comfortable than the cot I slept on the night before, he muttered to himself as he drifted into sleep. *And best of all, no Official Edwards.*

I t was well past two in the afternoon when Jacob awoke. For the first time in months he wasn't stiff. Even his second-hand couch was more comfortable than his prison cot. Not that he didn't still have plenty of aches and pains from Official Edwards' little goodbye party. *Now for a hot shower*, he thought. He never felt completely clean with the lukewarm water of the jail sink. He turned on the shower, allowed the water to reach a comfortably hot temperature, and washed off 90 days' worth of cell dust and disappointment in himself.

He considered his next move while drying off.

First, I have to find out about my truck and how much it will cost to get it out of impound.

Jacob dressed and started for the door. Out of habit, on the way out he glanced at the small table at the entryway of his apartment where he normally emptied his pockets. There sat a set of keys—his keys. He picked them up and stared at them.

What the heck?

He opened his front door and scanned the row of cars in the parking lot. Sitting in its assigned space was his beat-up Chevy truck. Jacob struggled to keep his mouth closed.

How did it get there? Did I drive back from the jail and not remember?

Jacob stepped out of his apartment and allowed the warmth of the Summer sun to penetrate his skin, relishing the warmth he hadn't felt in three months. His cold, dark, musty cell had no window to the outside world, the single opening to his cell permitting only the faux light from the prison hallway to filter through. That pale light didn't give off any semblance of heat. A playful summer breeze kicked the leaves into an impromptu dance around the walkway. Jacob closed his eyes, drew in a deep breath of fresh, free air, and allowed a long absent smile to crease his face.

A familiar voice startled him.

"Hey there buddy, how's it goin'?"

Jesse, his best friend—his only friend before his incarceration. After Mr. Ingles passed, they slowly lost contact, mostly due to his sudden decline into negativity. *No one wants to hang around with a cynic*, Jacob reminded himself.

"Jesse? What are you doing here? How did you even know I was home?"

"People talk," Jesse shrugged, brushing a lock of his jet-black hair out of his face. "I just happened to be listening."

Jacob extended his hand for a shake, but Jesse grabbed it and pulled him into a bearhug. "Seriously, dude. I was worried about you. When Renae told me about your arrest, I feared the worst. I know how those Officials can be."

"Uh, yeah. It wasn't a particularly pleasant experience," Jacob acknowledged. He pointed at his parking spot, "Are you the one who brought my truck?"

"No, that was Renae. After you were arrested, she saw that you left the keys in the ignition. She was ticked at you, but didn't want your car to get impounded. Before the Official could have it towed, she pulled it into her dad's garage. She drove it here the next day. She said she dropped the keys inside on your side table where you always kept them."

Well, that explains where the money went. Jacob put two and two together. *Renae knew of the coffee can. Heck, it was her idea back when we first got married. We used to keep one on the top shelf of our home—when it was still our home.* "Yeah, I have the keys." Jacob shows them in his hand. "I was about to leave for the impound yard when I saw them."

"Well, now that your schedule is cleared, we can grab some lunch. You haven't eaten yet, have you?"

Jacob thought back to last night's Hungry Man feast. "No, I haven't. Honestly, I just woke up. I am a little hungry."

"Great, I'll drive."

Jacob paused to lock the apartment door, then turned to follow his friend. When Jesse unlocked the passenger door of a new GMC Denali, he whistled in surprise. It was black with chrome trim that reflected the sunlight, resulting in an angelic glow.

"Nice ride. Where did you steal it from?"

"Bought it a month or so ago," Jesse said. "Much has happened in your absence, my friend. My new job keeps me busy, but the pay is good."

"Very nice," Jacob admits. "You've done well for yourself. What do you…?"

"So, where do you want to go?" Jesse interrupts. "Maggie's? No, I know—Dunham's. I bet you are just aching for a steak."

"Yeah, that sounds great." Jacob buckled his seat belt and relished the sound of radio blasting an old Journey tune. *Don't stop… Believin'. Hold on to that feeleeeaannn.*

"New truck, old music," Jacob murmured.

"Can't beat the classics. Plus, everyone likes Journey," Jesse responded. "It's like I've always said, there are two types of people; those who love Journey, and…"

"Liars," they both said in unison. And laughed.

Dunham's was an old-fashioned Steak House. The small town of Carrelton didn't offer much of a choice in restaurants. Other than Dunham's, there was Maggie's, a greasy spoon just off Interstate 37 known for a pretty good chicken fried steak. Truckers often stopped there on their way to the coast delivering their goods to the big box stores. Jacob, having been a trucker, spent enough time in greasy spoons to know a place like Dunham's was a real treat. Sometimes, on his shorter hauls for Mr. Anderson delivering sod, he would stop in if his load wasn't quite ready. He enjoyed being a trucker. Well, had enjoyed it—for a little while at least.

†††

Jacob grew up loving trucks. The big rigs he saw driving through town excited him. After high school, when college just wasn't working for him, he responded to an ad in the local newspaper and gave it a shot. Knowing he would need a commercial license; he went to the DPS office and grabbed a Drivers Handbook.

Getting a CDL permit involved passing several tests. You had to pass each section of the handbook before moving on to the next. Jacob went back to his car and studied the first chapter; General Knowledge. He walked back in, took the test, and passed. Back to his car, study, take the next test, repeat. He kept at it until he passed each test and was issued a permit. A short stint at A-Masters Trucking School and, *voila!* he received his CDL.

He started driving for a freight relocation company, moving

larger items, like pianos and armoires, that people didn't want to move in a U-Haul. He picked the items up at the old house and delivered them to the new. Sometimes it was interstate driving. He enjoyed that—cross country in three days. He felt like Cledus Snow in *Smokey and the Bandit*.

That job was short lived.

Jacob had a tradition regarding his parents' death anniversary. He did not work on that day. Jacob's boss wanted him to make a run that would overlap that date, and rejected his day-off request.

Jacob called him a name, questioning the legitimacy of his birth.

His boss called him unemployed.

Soon he found a job hauling sod from a farm on the other side of the county to just north of San Antonio where they were constructing new homes. He was paid by the pallet, so he tried to load up the flatbed twice a day. Sixteen pallets a load, 32 pallets a day, 15 dollars a pallet—$480 a day. *Not bad for a 20-year-old without a college degree*, he thought. Then Mr. Anderson retired, and his son took over. He cut the payrate to $5 per pallet. An argument ensued. Jacob quit—loudly. That was his last job as a trucker.

✝✝✝

Dunham's hit the spot. After three months of protein-enriched gruel, a thick, juicy steak was just what he needed. Especially after four frozen meals. As he and Jesse caught up, Jacob felt that now was the time to apologize to Jesse for his previous rude and obnoxious behavior toward him.

"When you're alone for three months you have time to think," Jacob began. "You've known me forever, Jesse. You were there for me when my parents died. If it wasn't for you, I don't think I could have made it through that junior year, much less our senior year. Their deaths showed me that time is short; that we're not guaranteed our next breath, and I didn't want anything to be left unsaid. But I let it get out of hand, and I became…"

"A pompous ass," Jesse finished.

"Yeah," Jacob admitted. "That's a pretty good description. I just want to say I am sorry, and I ask your forgiveness."

Jesse paused with his fork halfway between his plate and his mouth. The Jacob he knew three months ago would never apologize for anything. He lowered his fork, wiped his mouth and stared at his friend for a long moment.

"What did they do to you in there, Jake?"

Now it was Jacob's turn to laugh. "It's not what you think," he explained. "*They* did a lot, but that's not what caused the change in me. I met a man in the cell next to me. His name is Eric. He told me a lot of stuff—about God, and forgiveness. For the first time, it's like I can see, like my eyes have been opened to all the wrong I have done, all the hurt I've caused to those around me, to those I love; even to my closest relationships, like you. And Renae. I still don't know how I'm going to face her. You're a brother to me, and I know I've been a jerk. All I can do is ask for your forgiveness."

"Ok, I forgive you, Jake." Jesse said it almost as if he were afraid of the word. "So, are you like, a Christian now?"

Jacob paused and thought about it for a second, then smiled, "Yes, I guess you could say that I am. I never thought much about God before I was in lock-up. But it gave me a lot of time to think, ya know? Have you ever given God any thought?" Jacob felt odd for even asking such a question. He'd blurted it out without even thinking.

"I don't know, Jake. I guess you can say that I have known too many Christians. Either they are quiet and reserved and removed from anything seriously fun, or they are thumpin' you over the head with a Bible, telling you to *turn or burn*."

"Well, Eric was neither of those. He was polite and non-confrontational. He showed me a different side of who God is. And showed me that even a destructive man like myself could be made new."

Their conversation was interrupted by their waitress asking if they needed anything else.

"Just the check, darlin'," Jesse said with a wink.

She winked back and said, "Be right back with it, sweetie."

"Now, don't go thinking for a minute that you are paying, Jake," Jesse replied.

Jacob didn't push any further. He could see Jesse was uncomfortable with the God-talk. A secret smile played across his face, though, as he realized that for perhaps the first time in his life he didn't *want* to force the issue. He didn't have that urge to *say what needed saying*.

This must be how Eric felt, he thought. *Putting the words out there and letting God speak through that. Man, I miss that guy. I can't wait to see him when he's released next month.*

Jesse paid the check, and they left the restaurant. Jacob enjoyed Dunham's old-fashioned appearance and gazed at the aged photos of barns and windmills, shelves with rusted tin coffee cans and antique coke bottles, old road signs advertising Mobil Oil and Coke for 5 cents. Above the front door was a section of a fence; a gate—a five-barred gate. He smiled and thought of Ms Reimer, and his spoon-drawn collection of five-barred gates carefully etched into the wall of his now vacant cell.

Jacob arrived back home shortly before 6:00 p.m. The sun hung low on the horizon, casting an orange glow over his apartment building, making it appear engulfed in flames. He waved goodbye to Jesse, unlocked the front door, walked inside and dropped his keys on the small entryway table. They landed with a loud clank, which echoed through the apartment, underscoring its emptiness.

He pondered the countless times he had come home from work to have Renae greet him with a warm embrace and a tender kiss—back when their home was his home. The home he left; that he gave up to her, for Michael's sake.

The urge to talk to Renae was overwhelming. Instinctively he reached for his cellphone, then remembered it wasn't there. He wondered if perhaps it might still be his truck. Grabbing the keys from the table, he walked back to the truck to find out. The non-descript, older model Chevy sat stoically in its parking place. He bought it for getting around town because Renae needed their Civic to get to her job at the bank and to take Michael to daycare. Carrelton, a small town, just over 8,000 people, didn't have much in the way of public transportation, and he needed some wheels.

The truck was covered in a decent coat of pollen and dust. He slipped the key into the lock and twisted. The lock popped up and he pulled the handle. The door groaned open with a familiar creak, and the musty smell of warm car sitting in the Texas summer sun greeted him. There was no phone on the seat or on the dash, but a phone charger was plugged into the cigarette lighter. He followed the cord to the center console and pressed the release button. A smile crossed his face. There was his phone, fully charged.

A quick look erased his smile. *A half-dozen missed calls and a few text messages. Three months in lock-up, and that's all?* Reality crashed in. Jacob realized exactly how much he had been missed—and it wasn't much.

He sat in the driver's seat of the hot pickup cab and stared at his phone. Amid the aroma of stale car, there was still a hint of Renae's perfume.

He scrolled through the missed call log—a few from Renae, a couple from Jesse, the car insurance company. Most of the texts were from Renae. They began right after his arrest.

'Where are you? What happened? They aren't telling me where you are.'

'Jacob, the Carrelton Police say they do not have you in custody. You need to call me.'

'Jacob, I don't know why you are ignoring my texts. I need you to watch Michael. The daycare is closed today.'

The messages continued for a couple of weeks. At the end, they got heated. Then they stopped.

I guess she finally heard.

He started to text.

'Hey, Renae. It's Jake. I'd like to talk with you if it's—'

The phone starts ringing. It was Renae.

"Hey, I was just texting you," Jacob says.

"Really? I was wondering when you were going to finally contact me." Renae's voice had a cautious tone to it.

"Yes, I was released yesterday"

"Are you at your apartment?"

"Yes, I just got back. I was with Jesse," Jacob paused, not sure what he wanted to say. "Thank you for bringing my truck." *And thank you for taking the only money I had to my name.* He wanted to add.

"No problem. How are you?"

"Fine. I guess. It was an experience." Jacob rubbed the side of his cheek, which was still tender from his final paper signing. "I have a lot to tell you. Can we get together sometime?"

"I'm busy tonight, maybe tomorrow."

"How's Michael?"

"He's good. Running all over the place; like the Energizer Bunny now. It's hard to get him to slow down sometimes."

"I'd like to see him too."

"We'll see, Jacob. Step by step." There was an awkward pause that neither knew how to fill. "Look, I got to go," Renae said at last. "I just heard you were out, and I wanted to try and call you. Wasn't sure if you still had your phone or not. I will talk to you in the morning."

"Okay."

"Good night, Jacob."

"Good night, Renae. I miss you," he tried to add, but she had already hung up.

Jacob trudged back to his apartment, trying to process the conversation. *She called me. That's a positive, right? I mean, she was the one reaching out. It's not like I was harassing her or being needy. That's good, right? She said she'd talk to me tomorrow. What am I going to say to her? Where do I even begin?* He shook his head in amusement. *For someone who loves to speak his mind, you're sure picked a dandy time to draw a blank.*

Jacob sat on the couch and considered how his habit had gotten so out of hand. Renae once told him it was his frankness that attracted her to him. After Mr. Ingles passed away he became obsessed with the brevity of life and felt the compulsion to cling to anything he felt was important. At the top of that list was Renae. He loved her and wanted to spend his life with her. *Why should I wait any longer?* he had reasoned. Time was short, so he proposed. She said yes, and they got married.

But time was still his enemy—an enemy he met head-on in the only way he knew how; Delay nothing. That was especially true when it came to his words. *If it needs saying, I say it*, became his mantra, his own personal Code of the West.

Sometimes it worked out well. He was free with his compliments. He made sure to say *thank you*, even for the smallest of favors. His words were positive, uplifting, and people were encouraged.

But Jacob was equally free with his opinion when he felt something, or someone, needed correction.

It started with a polite suggestion to Jesse that he needed to quit smoking. Jesse didn't want to hear it. If he thought there was a better way to perform a particular household chore, he let Renae know she was doing it wrong. And he didn't limit his corrective discourse to friends and family. If the boss wanted him to perform a particular task in a particular way that happened to be different from the way Jacob thought the task should be performed, Jacob was quick to point out that the boss was obviously ill-informed, wrong, or just plain stupid.

Jacob shook his head as the memories flooded back. *It's no wonder Jesse stopped hanging around as much, or that I couldn't keep a job.*

With his best friend out of the picture, Renae and Michael were all Jacob had. Still, he hadn't recognized that he was likely the source of his own frustrations. He continued to spew his venom toward Renae. The night he was laid off was the last straw for her. She left and took Michael with her. It dawned on him, perhaps for the first time, that it was his words that made her cry. Then she was gone. He was left with nothing.

Tears rolled down Jacob's cheek. He brushed them away with the back of his hand, hating the way he was feeling, but incapable of staunching the flow of emotion. All the pain of what he put Renae through washed over him like a rising tide. He felt her loneliness, her confusion, her sense of helplessness against his raging verbal attacks. He yearned to go back in time and make things right. But the past was the past. Tears could not wash that away. He somehow had to deal with the present, and he pondered how to do that.

First step—apologize. Eric taught me that much. Not that it would fix anything or cause her to leap into my arms, but it's a start.

He blew out a long breathe. Apologizing to Jesse was easy. He was a friend. And he was a guy. And he had already made the first move by taking him to lunch. Renae was a whole different set of challenges. She was a woman. That by itself was a minefield just waiting for a misstep. She had also been his wife. Their relationship was on a completely different level than friendship. And of all the people he had hurt, she was the one who endured the most.

Wish I could talk to Eric right now. He'd know what to do.

Emotionally drained, Jacob laid back on the couch and stared at the ceiling, thinking of the connect-the-dots on his cell ceiling, and feeling a bit like a stranger in a strange land. At least in jail he didn't have to make decisions about what to do with his life. *It's amazing how fast you can become accustomed to being controlled*, he pondered. *Eric is in for a whole year. I can't imagine what he's going through. He still has another month—30 more spoon lines, six more five-barred gates.*

Jacob smiles. Soon Eric will be released. It's the only thought that offers any comfort to his roiled spirit. All the uncertainty of the coming days just makes him afraid. Jacob drifted into slumber, wondering if he'll even recognize Eric once he is released. After all, he's never even seen his face.

Morning announced itself with an incessant banging on the front door. Startled, Jacob fumbled awake, looking around for a bowl of gruel in the dim light. It took him a moment to remember where he was. A level of calm returned once he remembered he was home. He stretched and sat up, enjoying a moment of peace before reality crashed in. *No wife in bed beside you, no child noises over a baby monitor, no job. This is my new normal.* Jacob stumbled to the bathroom sink and filled a paper cup with water. He rinsed out his mouth, then splashed his face, trying to shake the dream that awakened him.

The pounding came again. Jacob's eyes widened. It wasn't a dream that woke him.

"I know you're in there, citizen," the familiar voice calls out.

Edwards?! What the...

Jacob padded down the hallway in his pajama bottoms and bare feet. He leaned forward to peer through the peephole, but the only thing he can see a veil of smoke. A rogue breeze blows the vapors away to reveal the grumpy, wrinkled face of his recent nemesis. Pins and needles jabbed the length of Jacob's spine. *What could he want?*

"Open up, or I'll break it down!"

"Alright, alright. Give me a second," Jacob called out as he fumbled with the deadbolt.

"I'm in a generous mood; you have two seconds, citizen."

Jacob cracked open the door. Edwards stood there in his whites, his signature cigar clenched between his teeth. "What took you so long?" he mumbled around the cigar. It came out sounding something like, *whaa hoo yoo hao haung?* Jacob's confused expression registered, and Edwards pulled the cigar from his mouth and added, "What are you hiding?"

"Nothing Official. I'm sorry for the delay. I was asleep." Jacob unlatched the safety change and opened the door wider., "What can I do for you, Official Edwards?"

"I just wanted to be sure you were keeping on the straight and narrow, Mr. Andrews. Remember that I am watching you. One false move and I will put your ass back in that cell and unfind the key."

I must have really offended this guy. Was it the 'glorified hall monitor' comment, or my stomping on his foot?

Edwards pushed passed Jacob and wandered around his living room, his nose crinkling in disapproval. "Whatever it is you're planning, it won't work," Edwards said at last.

"I'm sorry, Official. I'm not sure I know what you're talking about. I don't have anything planned, other than trying to see my son." A sudden fear tripped Jacob's brain. "Did Renae call you? Did she say I had done something wrong, because I've barely spoken to her and I didn't say anything —"

"Your business with your ex-wife is none of my concern right now, citizen," Edward sneered as if he knew some deep dark secret and was ready to pounce. "You know damn well what I'm talking about. Don't think I don't know what you and Lassiter are up to. He is going to know for damn sure that it's not going to work. He will receive special instructions as to what is expected when he is released next month. I'm here to make sure that you understand as well. I don't want to have to give you special instructions as well. Consider this a… friendly… consultation."

"Friendly. Yes sir, Official. Understood." Jacob's old nature rebelled, demanding to speak, but Jacob's better sense shoved the retort down.

Edwards eyes shot open beneath his furry gray eyebrows, "You mocking me, citizen?"

"No sir. Of course not, sir. I wouldn't do that, sir. I've learned my lesson and require no further instruction." Jacob is serious. Not only did he not want to go back to jail, he truly did not want to return to the man he used to be.

Edwards pointed his cigar at Jacob's nose. "I have my eye on you, citizen."

As Edward turned to leave, Jacob called after him, "Official Edwards, I am genuinely sorry for what I said to you when we first met. It was wrong for me to challenge you like I did. For that, I apologize."

Edwards turned back, and squished look of confusion on his face. "Hmmph," was his only reply. Taking long drag off his cigar, he blew the smoke in Jacobs direction, then marched back to his truck.

Jacob closed and locked the door, then collapsed onto his couch. "Wow, didn't see that coming," he muttered aloud. The light on his cellphone was blinking—missed call from Renae. He checked his voice mail.

"Hey Jacob, it's Renae. I'm going to be in San Antonio most of the morning. If you still want to meet we'll have to make it quick. I can meet you at Maggie's around 2. I won't have Michael with me though. I'll see you then. Bye."

Hearing her voice puts a smile on his face. Even when

agitated, her voice had a soothing effect. It was just one of the many things he loved about her—one of the many things he never told her he loved about her. *That's all going to change.*

It dawned on Jacob that even though he had lived his life trying to not miss opportunities, he was missing some of the most important opportunities of his life. *How did I let it get this far? All I wanted to do was make sure there was never the regret of words unsaid. Oh, Renae, I'm so sorry.*

†††

The truck stop was always busy with truckers from all over South Texas drawn to the dive by the addictive aroma of chicken fried steak. Jacob entered to the sound of dishes clanking, chicken frying, and truckers sharing stories of the road. A familiar voice called out. "Jacob? Jacob Andrews? Is that you?"

"Hey, Margaret," Jacob waved.

"Where ya been sweetie? Haven't seen you in months?"

Jacob figured the question was rhetorical. Margaret would have heard by now. Everyone would have heard by now. This was a small town; Maggie's served as its temple of Chisme, and Margaret served as its unofficial high priestess. In Carrelton, gossip was treated as a national pastime and Margaret was more than willing to do her part to keep everyone informed of everyone else's business.

"Around," Jacob explained.

"Well, have a seat, and I'll fix ya somethin' up."

"Is Renae here?"

Haven't seen her. You expectin' her?"

"Yes, I must have beaten her here."

"Well, sit anywhere you please. Water?"

"Yes, thank you." Jacob sat in a booth with a view of the

parking lot so he could see when she pulled up. Margaret set a plastic tumbler full of ice water in front of him and wandered away to tend to other customers. He pondered what he wanted to say between sips.

Fifteen minutes and two glasses of water later a dark green Civic pulled up to an open space at the far end of the lot. *Here she comes.* Jacob's heart skipped a beat as he watched her, sitting in the car for several minutes. He was afraid she would change her mind and simply drive away, and prayed she wouldn't.

At last her door opened and she stepped out. Her beauty took his breath away, and he remembered how he felt the first time he saw her. He cursed himself mentally for all the stupid, thoughtless things he'd said to her; things that hurt, things that demeaned, things that crushed her spirit.

She walked toward the diner alone. True to her word, she hadn't brought Michael. In a way Jacob was relieved. *If a thing needs saying, I need to say it*, he thought, only this time, what needed saying, truly did need saying. He wanted her full attention while he said what he had to say. He needs to mend things with Renae before adding Michael to the mix.

Renae walked through the door of the truck stop looking like an angel. She wore a black skirt with a red floral design and a black blouse that accentuated her figure. The wind wafted through her auburn hair, teasing it into her face and getting it tangled in her sunglasses.

She is breathtaking.

Renae paused at the entrance, lifted her sunglasses, and looked around. She spotted Jacob and walked toward his table, but her expression never changed. If she was glad to see him, he couldn't tell.

"Hi," Jacob said. He had spent the better part of the past two days rehearsing what he would say when he saw Renae. What came out was, *hi*. He shook his head. She had him speechless.

"Hi," she echoed.

"Can you sit down?"

Renae nodded after a considered pause. "I can't stay long. I have to get back to work."

"I understand. How is Michael?"

"Good. He's running all over the place."

"Can I see him?"

"Jake, are we going to go through this again, because—"

"I'm sorry," Jacob held up his hand to gently cut her off. "I'm not trying to argue. As you said, all in due time."

She raised an eyebrow, surprised by his composure. "Thank you."

"How are you? How's the bank and the new position? Well, maybe not so new now."

"I'm growing into it. Occasionally I have a problems with the tellers under me, but I'm finding my way."

"Good. I'm glad." Jacob smiled as he gazed into her green eyes. They always mesmerized him.

"What?" she asked, unsure of the intent behind his smile.

"I've missed you, Renae."

"Look," she started, refusing to meet his eyes. "There is something you need to know."

This can't be good, he thought, but remained silent, waiting.

"Jacob," Renae fumbled with trying to find the right words. "You may not know this; I'm sure you don't know, or we wouldn't be having this conversation." She paused and drew in a deep breath. "Look, there's no easy way to say this, so

I'm going to come right out and say it. For the last month or so I've been kinda seeing someone."

"What?!"

"Jake, you have to understand. I thought you were dead."

"Wait. Dead? How? Why?" he stumbled over his words. "What would make you think I was dead?"

"I was told you were being taken to the county lock-up. I put your truck in daddy's garage to keep them from towing it, and a day or so later I drove it back to your place. I let myself in so I could leave the keys inside. You have to understand how angry I was with you. I went through some of your things, and I found your coffee can, just like the one we used to keep at the house. So… I took the money from it to help with Michael. A week later I get a call saying that you were killed while trying to escape."

Jacob forced his jaw closed. He sat stunned for a long moment before he could find any words to say.

"Who called you?" he said at last. "Who told you I was dead?"

"I don't remember his name. I was too upset. Edwin, Eldridge, something like that."

"Edwards?"

"I don't know. Maybe." A tear leaked down her face and trickled off her chin.

Jacob nodded, trying to control his emotions and stifle the raging of his old nature.

"And who are you… seeing?"

"He's been a friend to me, Jacob. He was there through most of what happened after we separated. Then he was there after you were arrested. And, he was there when word came that you were dead."

"Well, obviously, as you can clearly see, I am not dead."

"Yes, obviously. When Daddy heard that you were being released, he called me. As you can imagine, I was in shock. You were gone. You were dead. I had reconciled myself to that. Then to hear you're alive? And to see you—alive? I'm confused and I don't even know how I'm supposed to feel."

"Renae, who are you seeing?"

Jacob wasn't sure what name he expected to hear, but it wasn't the one Renae said. His heart shattered into a million pieces when she said. "I'm involved with Jesse. Jesse Durrant."

The last month has been brutal for Jacob. After Renae dropped her bombshell on him they had spoken exactly twice. The first time she told him she didn't think it was a good idea for him to see Michael yet. The second time she said he could see his son, but only at her house, under supervision, and only for a brief visit.

He missed his son. He missed his wife. It tore him apart to think about the woman he loved in the arms of another man. It hurt even worse to know the arms of that other man belonged to his former best friend. *What was up with that whole visit from Jesse? He knew what was going on. He was already involved with Renae. He also knew she thought he was dead. And to buy him lunch and act like nothing had changed? It doesn't add up.*

Something wasn't right. He just couldn't put his finger on it.

Jacob sat at his kitchen table nursing a steaming cup of coffee. With each sip he pondered the realities of his new normal. "This is my life now," he muttered aloud as he allowed the caffeine to work its magic. The sound of a weed eater trimming the overgrown grass around his walkway reminded him of the nuisance of the lawn at his house—at what used to be his house, the house he'd shared with Renae and their son. Seemed like every time he turned around that yard needed cutting or weeding. It always grew so fast. *Not my problem*, he mused. *Not anymore.*

It had been 29 days since his release from prison—5 five-barred gates plus four. He would cross of the sixth batch today. That meant Eric would be released soon; today or tomorrow. He couldn't wait. He knew it was selfish, but he needed his friend to talk to, to give him some sage advice.

He glanced at the clock on the kitchen wall, and nearly swore. It was later than he expected. If he didn't hit the road immediately, he'd be late for work. He'd picked up a job running parts for the local hardware/auto parts store. It didn't pay much, but it was a job. It put food on the table, paid the rent, and provided a few other luxuries he had taken for granted before his arrest.

He worked four days a week, eight to 10 hours a day, depending on whether he needed to run up to New Braunfels to get a part from their distributor. Most of the time the local hub had the part, but if a customer needed his item quick, Jacob got the privilege of heading up Interstate 35. He didn't mind. He enjoyed the solitude of driving, plus the company paid mileage for road trips. Win-win.

Jacob grabbed his keys and headed out the door a few minutes before 9. Once outside his apartment complex he noticed a large black pickup behind him. Every turn Jacob made, the truck made as well. He started to get a little paranoid, and made a sudden turn into the McDonald's parking lot. The truck slowed, but didn't follow. It did turn into the parking lot of the bank next door. *Maybe the guy just happened to be going the same direction,* he reasoned, feeling a bit more relaxed. But while he sat in his truck watching, the other driver never opened his door. The old anxiety rose inside of Jacob again.

A long hedge separated the two lots, and Jacob made a quick plan. He got out of his truck and strolled into the McDonald's without looking around. He walked straight through to the other side and exited the building, trotted around behind the building, skirted the hedges, and stealthily made his way to the passenger side. The windows were tinted dark, so he couldn't see inside. Anger and frustration finally won out, and Jacob pounded on the window.

"Why are you following me?" Jacob demanded.

The driver, obviously concentrating on the restaurant entrance, startled, threw the truck into reverse and almost knocked Jacob down as it peeled out of the parking lot. Jacob was unable to identify the driver, but the truck looked awfully familiar. And he could hear the radio playing classic rock.

Jacob made his way back to his truck and took a quick glance at the clock. *Crap. I'm gonna be late.* He drove as fast as the law would allow. It wasn't fast enough.

Stan was a 'git 'er done' kind of boss; the kind who fervently believed 10 minutes early was on time, on time was late, and time was money. The did not like tardiness, and he liked excuses even less. He didn't even look up when Jacob ran in.

"I'm sorry, I'm sorry, I'm sorry," Jacob apologized. "I had car trouble, and…"

"It's 9:45."

"I know."

"You're late."

"I know."

"I need to run up to New B and pick up an alternator for Roger over at Mills Motors." Stan shoved the invoice at him. "I need it back here by one o'clock."

"One o' clock? But it's already, 9:45—"

"9:48. And whose fault is that? I need it back here by one," he repeated. "Hit the highway and pedal to the metal, son."

"I'm already there, boss." That was Carrelton Hardware and Auto's unofficial slogan; 'We're already there.' Jacob scanned the parking lot for a big Denali. Nothing. He blew out a sigh of relief.

Jacob pushed it to just over the speed limit, fast enough to make up some precious time, but not fast enough to attract the attention of Smokey Bear. The last thing he needed was to draw the interest of the county sheriff, state troopers, or heaven forbid any Officials. Just as he reached New Braunfels his cell phone buzzed. It was Stan.

"Hey, the part is not in the distributor's warehouse. It's over at Johnny's Auto Body on Highway 46. Address is on the invoice."

"Got it. I'm not far." The address was on the other side of the highway, but only required a couple of turns. A dilapidated metal sign that read 'John uto S op' stood at the entrance to a gate with the street number painted in dull black letter. *Ain't no place like this place, so This must be the place,* he reasoned as he turned into the drive.

The gate to the shop was closed, but there was a rusted sign with a big red arrow pointing down. The sign read, Push for Service. He pushed the button below the arrow. While he waited for a response, he was startled to realize the gate to Johnny's was a five-barred gate. *Coincidence?* He pondered. *Seems like that emblem just keeps showing up in my life lately.* A crackly buzz jarred him from his reverie, and a static-filled voice came across an intercom system attached to a rusted pole.

"Drive on up to the shop," the voice said.

Jacob followed the dirt path up to what looked like an old barn or stable; he assumed it was the shop. A middle-aged man in grease-stained coveralls wiped his hands on a rag and shook his hand as he got out of his pickup. "You here for the alternator?"

"Yes, sir. I'm with Carrelton Hardware and Auto."

"You must be Jacob." The man said, adjusting his Pennzoil ball cap.

"Yes, sir."

"I've heard much about you, my friend. "My name is William Johnson."

"Nice to meet you, Mr. Johnson."

"Call me Will. Or William, if you simply have to be formal."

"Okay, Will." Jacob cocked an eyebrow at the older man. "Do we know each other?"

"No, not quite. Follow me." Will led him into the stable.

Jacob's eyebrows climbed up to his hairline. What appeared to be a dilapidated old stable on the outside was a clean, modern full-service mechanic shop on the inside. Concrete floor with a cellar for oil changes. Chrome everywhere. Walls of parts. And much like Dunham's, classic old advertising signs for everything from Burma Shave to ESSO Oil decorated the walls. "This is amazing. Looking at the outside you'd… I mean… I didn't mean to…" Jacob stuttered.

"Thank you," Will laughed. "I get that a lot. I'm glad the work I've done here is appreciated." Will looked at his clipboard, squinted, then extended his arm. At last he gave up and reached into his shirt pocket for a pair of reading glasses. His finger followed down a list, and he smiled when he found what he was looking for. "Lot 3, Section 2" He looked up at the wall, "Ah yes, here it is."

Jacob signed for the part, and they headed out to his truck. The air had shifted from the north, bringing a chill to it.

"Front's moving in," Will said.

"That's what the weatherman said. Sorry, the weather*person*. Hope I didn't offend you."

Jacob climbed into the cab of his truck, and Will reached in through the window and shook his hand, holding it a bit longer than normal. His rich brown eyes met Jacobs and he said, "You know Jacob, there are more of us than you may realize. We're all in this together. Do not fear, my brother."

Will released his grasp and walked away. As Jacob started the engine, Will hollered over his shoulder, "Say hello to Eric for me," then disappeared into his shop.

Jacob left New Braunfels at 11:50. He had just over an hour to get the part to Mills Motors back in Carrelton. *Wow. That was weird.* He pulled out his phone and called the shop. "Stan, do you know anything about this order from Johnny's Auto?"

"All I know is that you have less than an hour to get your butt back here. Remember, we never miss a delivery time. *Never.*"

"Thank you, sir. I'm already there. But, there weren't any special instructions?"

"Only that they requested you. Said you had been up to his shop before and only wanted to deal with you."

Weirder and weirder.

"Who ordered the part?"

"It was Jessica over at Mills Motors," Stan said. "They need it for an old Buick they were working on for a customer."

"Did she tell you the customer's name?"

"What do I look like, the Answer Man? You're paid to drive, not ask questions."

"Seriously, Stan. This is important."

"Alrightalright. Don't get your knickers in a twist. Paper-work says the part is for some guy named Eric Lassiter. Now get a move on. I don't want to hear your voice unless you're calling to tell me you made the delivery on time. 'Cause we never miss a delivery time."

Jacob's foot hit the gas pedal. "I'm already there."

J acob was so focused on reaching his destination that he failed to notice the large black pickup that was four cars behind him. Or the silver Denali that followed behind the back one. The silver Denali took a crossover and headed back north toward New Braunfels. When Jacob did notice the black one in his rear-view mirror, his heart skipped a beat. But he slowed down and the pickup turned and drove away in the opposite direction. *False alarm.*

Jacob pulled into Mills Motors at two minutes past one, and sprinted into the office where a twenty-something girl with dark brown hair and piercing hazel eyes greeted him with a smile. "Hey Jacob, you made it! On time, as usual."

"Not quite, a few minutes late," Jacob squirmed. Jessica pointed over to the clock on the wall. "Not according to our official records. The clock read 12:58. She smiled and cupped her hand beside her lips and mouthed *'It's five minutes slow. Our little secret.'*

Jacob grinned and mouthed, *'Thank you.'* Out loud he said, "Here is the part you ordered." He handed her the box containing the part and the invoice to sign, ,then added, "Is… um… Is the customer here?"

"Not yet. Roger is supposed to install this and then give him a call." She looked down at her agenda, "Pick-up time set at 6:30 for Mr. Lassiter."

"Do you know Mr. Lassiter?"

"Oh, yes, he's a long-time customer, although he hasn't been in for a while. His Buick has been back in storage for nearly a year now. We just recently found his part. Guess they don't make them like they used to. Do you know him?"

Jacob smiled. "Yes, I know him." Then he added, "I've never actually seen him, but I know him." Jessica shot him a quizzical look, which made him laugh. "I'll see you later, Jessica. Have a blessed day."

"Ok, Jake. I'll see you next order."

Jacob was walking on air. At least now he knew when they would finally meet face-to-face—tonight, at a 6:30. His joy quickly turned to concern. *Wonder what type of shape Eric is in? Given my own paper signing event, it could be back for Eric. And he's been in lock-up way longer than I was.*

Jacob had never been one to watch the clock. Truth be told, since he landed this job he was more likely to hang around looking for more hours. But today he was ready to leave work like a runner on the starting blocks. At a quarter till six he stood at the parts counter, tapping the pencil he was holding, staring at time clock watching the seconds tick by. Excitement mingled with concern for his friend's well-being coursed through him. It was finally time to pull back the curtain and see the man behind it. The big reveal at the end of a long story. It was time to meet his friend.

Memories of his first day out romped through his mind. He wondered if Eric would have the same experience. After his cryptic conversation with Will Johnson he wondered if perhaps Eric was already out? How else would he have ordered the part in the first place? Did they release him early? How would he know him when he saw him?

At one second past 6:00 p.m. he punch the clock and ran to his truck. He made the trek to Mills Motors, arriving at exactly 6:30—*6:25 inside time.* There was one shop bay open, and he could make out the tail of an older model Buick. He parked his pickup in the Service Department Only slot and walked over to the open bay. He could hear Roger under the hood, working with a socket wrench, cussing a stuck nut.

"Hey Roger."

Roger stepped out from under the hood. "Oh, hey, Jacob. Wasn't expecting you. What can I do for you?"

"I'm looking for the owner of this fine Buick."

"Jessica said he called and said he was running a bit late," Roger said, wiping his hands on a rag. "He should be along any time now."

"So, are you admiring my classic, Jacob?"

Jacob recognized the voice instantly, and he was almost too nervous to turn around. When he did, he saw a short, stocky man with a wide grin and an unexpected lack of hair. He was older than Jacob expected, but then again, he wasn't sure what he had expected.

"Eric?"

"Well, if I'm not, I'm about to drive away in his sweet ride." Eric opened his arms and pulled Jacob into a bear hug. "It's good to finally see you, Jacob. Really good."

"You look better than I expected," Jacob said, "considering my recent experience." Jacob looked Eric up and down, surprised at his apparently whole and healthy appearance. It seemed they didn't touch him at all. "I expected them to do a worse number on you than they did me."

"Edwards made his normal threats. The final week his look

changed. But I'll explain all of that later. How are we looking, Roger? She all fixed up?" Eric asked.

"I won't lie to you; she was a fighter, Mr. Lassiter. Especially after sitting the better part of a year. I did my best to remember to start her regularly like Mr. Johnson asked. I guess he had a heck of a time finding that part."

"As long as she is purring now. That's all I care about. Long time or short."

"She's running, don't know about purring. Her purr gave out 20 years ago. But she will get you around. I also did an oil change and tune-up, no charge."

"Why thank you." Then to Jacob, "See, that's why I've been coming here for years. They know how to take care of their customers. You're a blessing Roger, I appreciate it."

"No worries Mr. Lassiter," Roger said, closing the hood. "She's good to go. Keys are in the ignition."

"What do you say we head out of here," Eric said, grabbing Jacob on the shoulder. "I'm famished. Meet me at Maggie's?"

†††

Maggie's was always packed, but at night the clientele shifted to mostly long-haul truckers taking their 10-hour reset. When he drove delivering the sod, Jacob didn't have to 10-out during his shift; he never worked enough hours. But his boss always made sure he was compliant and kept accurate logbooks, even though legally he was exempt.

While the lot was full of big rigs, the diner was relatively empty. The dinner rush had already passed, and most of the business was cabbed up trying to get some sleep for an early call to hit the road again. Jacob and Eric pulled in together. *Roger was right*, Jacob thought. *Eric's Buick is far from purring.*

Not that I have anything to brag about. This old pickup has seen better days as well.

Margaret was front and center as they walked in. "Don't you ever take any time off, Maggs?" Jacob said.

"Oh sweetie, there'll be time for time-off when I'm dead," she jested. "You here to eat or socialize?"

"Most definitely eat," Eric said.

"How ya been, Eric? It's been a while." Margaret said.

"I'm holding my own. Just got back into town."

"Well, you two cuties take a seat, and I'll be right with you," she said with a wink, pointing to an empty booth.

After settling in and allowing the reality of their reunion wash over them for a few comfortable moments, Jacob asked, "Tell me, how did you get out that hell-hole without a scratch on you?"

"I honestly don't know. When I heard what the deputies were doing to you in the other room, I have to admit to a certain level of dread. I couldn't imagine I'd get less abuse than you suffered. But the strangest thing happened. It was the week prior to my release. I was summoned into Official Edwards office. He said he had something planned for me and that I shouldn't get too comfortable on the outside. He admonished me to remain quiet and to stop all this talk about God. He said that people didn't want to hear it, and since they didn't want to hear it, it was illegal for me to say it, and that if he caught me even thinking about speaking publicly again, he would deal with me on the spot."

"That's insane," Jacob said. After a moment's thought he added, "Can he do that?"

"He can *say* whatever he wants to. He's the Official. There are no recording devices or cameras in their offices. So, it would be my word against his. Remember, they are above reproach. They can hide behind a mask in public and show everyone how nice and polite they can be, but when you get one behind closed doors, you're in for a real treat."

"Isn't there anything you can do?"

"Not legally. Not since those laws went into effect." Eric hung his head, "How can we obey the Great Commission now? Going out and making disciples of all men can carry a death sentence. If we even say the word *sinner*, or even imply that a person might need to repent, and the wrong person gets wind of it, we are in a world of hurt."

Eric lowered his voice. "You do realize that just by having this conversation, we're putting ourselves in danger." Eric pointed at another table, "If that couple over there heard our conversation and took any offense whatsoever, they could report it, and we both would be back in those caverns. Or worse."

"I read this morning that more than half of the churches in Atlanta and surrounding areas have already closed their doors, and more are closing every day." Jacob said.

"It gets worse. State governments are recruiting their own Officials to help enforce the Anti-Dehumanization Act. In some states it goes way beyond just religion. It's now illegal to offend anyone about anything. There's a lawsuit in Indiana, where a woman was offended by the music being played in the car next to her. She copied down the license plate, and the driver, a woman in her seventies, is facing jail time. Ten years for listening to Wagner's Ring Cycle. It's beyond insane, Jacob." He lowered his voice even further. "There are those of us who feel something needs to be done. And done quickly—before it's too late."

Jacob nodded, understanding washing over him. A smile creased his lips and he said, "Oh, by the way, Will Johnson said to say hello."

"I'm glad that worked out," Eric returned his grin. "I took a chance that you'd be the one to go up there. Yes, I made the request."

"How long have you been out?"

"Long enough to find out where you were and what's been going on in the world."

"I've been so preoccupied with Renae and Michael, that honestly I've been pretty much oblivious to anything else that's going on. All I know is that I know I'm being followed. Edwards even visited me just to reinforce that he was keeping an eye on me. For all I know I'm being watched now."

"Denalis?"

"Yes, a black one. I've seen a white one as well," Jacob said.

"The white one is Edwards. Turner and Anderson drive a silver one. The black is one of his new deputies. I don't know who he is. I haven't seen him or caught his name."

The light suddenly dawned in Jacob's brain. *It all makes perfect sense now.* "I have a pretty good idea who he is." Bile rose in the back of his throat. "So, Eric, what do we do now? Will said there are more of us than I know."

Eric looked around and kept his voice low. "We make a stand. There are more of us than you know. Plenty of us, in fact to make a serious statement. I have access to a meeting place. We used to meet at Will's place, but I fear that location is now compromised. You went inside his shop, right?"

Jacob nodded.

"Then you may have seen the area for oil changes?"

Jacob nodded again.

"There is a secret room down there. It used to be for storage, but after I was arrested and my church closed, committee members would make the drive up to his place and meet there. I may have tipped my hand when I sent you up there. But I needed to get a message to you. It was the only way I could think of."

Jacob remembered seeing the silver Denali headed back North after meeting up with the black one. "I think Turner and Anderson went up there. I saw them."

"We can't delay any longer. He may be in trouble. We all may be. Texas used to be a safe place considering the state government is as much against the federal laws as we are, but Christianity as we know it is dying. There is no way we can survive if we don't band together."

"What do you need me to do?" Jacob had heard that same passion through a stone wall in prison. But to see the fire in Eric's eyes—that was enough for him. Jacob had spent the better part of his life verbally abusing people. He was amazed he hadn't end up in prison sooner. Now he realized there was a purpose behind the timing of his arrest, one not orchestrated by any Official of the government. He knew it was so he could meet Eric. The direction of God was at play here. And he was ready; ready to make his life count for something with words of encouragement instead of words of insult and degradation.

"Come with me, Jacob. I need to rebuild the church God assigned to me. I believe it's His plan for us to somehow make a difference. But we can't make a difference if we do not take a stand. I won't lie to you. It will be dangerous. Especially if these laws remain enforced. As long as there are Officials out there like Edwards, we can rest assured that our very lives are at stake.

"Like Paul, we will be tested and tried, maybe even persecuted publicly. Edwards will make it all appear legal, tied up with a pretty bow. So, you can get out now if you want. I won't hold it against you, but I feel we were brought together for a reason."

Eric paused. Looked deep into Jacob's eyes and asked, "Are you with me?"

Jacob broke the stare. He looked outside for a moment. Life went on outside as if the world wasn't burning. Trucks ran up and down the highway. People wandered in and out of the diner, oblivious to the future, their future, their freedom, which was being stripped away, bit by bit. And there was nothing they could do about it.

He believed what Eric was telling him. He believed it like nothing he has ever believed before.

"Yes, of course, I am with you. When do we begin?"

Eric smiled and said, "Now"

$$\text{卌 卌 ||}$$

Eric drove into the parking lot of the old high school. He had long since turned off his headlights, using only the moonlight for illumination. There was a carport ahead, hidden by overgrown brush, rubbish, and pieces of weathered plywood. *Good hiding place,* Jacob mused. *If you didn't know it was there you would miss it.*

"Where are we?" Jacob asked.

"Polk High School, or what remains of it. It's abandoned now. They closed it when the city system merged with the county. Kids have attended classes at the new high school ever since."

"I remember hearing about that. A lot of angry parents."

"Yes, I was one of them," Eric said.

"You must live around here, then?"

"Not too far."

Eric parked the rumbling Buick in an unobtrusive spot, then got out and laid a couple of branches across the rear. It wasn't a perfect camouflage job, but someone would have to be looking to see it. Satisfied, Eric led Jacob toward the buildings, skillfully guiding him through a maze of paths and brush. *He's done this before,* Jacob realized. It took a few moments for their eyes to adjust to the darkness, but enough moonlight streamed through the clouds to allow them to move swiftly. Mosquitoes and Cicadas buzzed about as they passed by one of the outer buildings of the old high school complex.

They used the fence line as a guide, and once they reached a closed gate, Eric pulled a key from his pocket to unlock it. It swung open on silent hinges and Eric strode through. Jacob stood planted, staring at the open five-barred gate.

"What's wrong?" Eric said.

"Nothing. It's just," Jacob paused and pointed at the gate, "It's just that I keep seeing those— everywhere. An old teacher of mine used to call that design a five-barred gate. While I was in prison, I kept track of my days by marking that design on my cell wall. Ever since I got out, I've been seeing them everywhere; Will's property, Dunham's Steakhouse, Mills Motors. Well, Mills' wasn't actually a gate. It was a pallet with some slats missing, but it formed that design. And now here."

Eric motioned for Jacob to follow, grinning like a Cheshire Cat. Jacob could almost hear a childish, sing-song voice chanting, "I know something you don't know!"

"What is it?" Jacob asked.

"There are more of us than you know," Eric answered.

"That's what Will said."

"Will, Roger, and Frank Dunham were all members of the church I pastored. They were deacons. Shortly before the church was closed and I was arrested, we began to meet here secretly—just the four of us. We discussed the situation and what we should do. I didn't want them to face the same persecution I was. We were all being watched by Officials. That symbol you keep seeing, the five-barred gate, we didn't plan it. I never even realized they all had that in common. But I believe God orchestrated it. I believe He used those gates to show you that you are on the right path."

Eric led the way to a large steel door toward the back of another large building. He took a quick look around, then raised a latch and opened the door to reveal a steep staircase leading down into the ground.

"Old bomb shelter," he explained as he pointed to the structure above. "Built under the auditorium. It's been here since the Cold War days. We're safe down there."

After closing the door, Eric hit a switch on the wall. A dim yellow glow flickered through fluorescent ceiling lights illuminated staircase into the far reaches of the shelter. The eerie closeness of the facility reminded Jacob of the caverns of the jail. The thought was not comforting.

"Before converting this into our meeting place, I had only been down here once," Eric talked as he walked. "I was in the auditorium when a tornado warning went off. They led us all down here. Before that I didn't even know this place existed. After the school closed, nobody thought much more about it. It's just another abandoned relic of the Cold War era. We decided to prep it for use—"

"In case of another storm," Jacob added.

"Yes. I knew I was going to be arrested eventually, I just didn't know when. Honestly, I didn't think it was going to be as soon as it was, but I wasn't going to back down. People need to know about the Lord and his saving grace, but you can't experience grace without recognizing the reality of sin. Once sin and grace are revealed, the Holy Spirit does the work."

"So, you continued to preach repentance?" Jacob said.

"That is the heart of the Gospel, so yes."

At the end of the hall they encountered another steel door. It opened with a creak to reveal a large room furnished with several fold-out tables and chairs. Posters of scenery with Bible verses lined the walls. One verse, *"Narrow is the gate,"* accented a painting of a five-barred gate, slightly opened. Jacob pointed at the picture. "I guess I'm in the right place."

Eric chuckled. He stepped to a wooden podium at the front of the room and picked up leather-bound binder, then indicated one of the folding tables where Jacob joined him. "I want to show you something." He pulled out a newspaper clipping and handed it to Jacob.

Jacob reads the headline aloud. "Atlanta man wins case over local church." He then read the rest of the story.

Atlanta, GA – George Mathis finally won his $2 million civil lawsuit on Wednesday over Our Savior's Cross Baptist Church. The lawsuit stemmed from a chance visit to the church six months ago. Mathis agreed to attend a Sunday Morning service at Our Savior's Cross Baptist Church at the invitation of a friend whose name is being withheld as per his request. Pastor of OSC, Eric Lassiter…"

Jacobs eyes nearly jumped out of his head. "That was you? You were the pastor?"

"Yes, I was." Eric nodded. "That lawsuit broke the church. There was no such thing as defamation insurance back then. To pay off the lawsuit, we had to sell everything. The building, the pews, my personal home, vehicles—everything. The denomination suffered through a huge barrage of negative publicity and soon severed ties with me. And with the media spotlight, even our town quickly became a pariah. Atlanta was ground zero for the new laws being proposed across the country. I could no longer speak freely in Georgia, and I was afraid for the safety of my family, so we relocated to Texas."

"That's crazy. So, you were there at the beginning," Jacob said.

"Yes. Yes, I was. Once that court decision was reached religious freedom went out the door. It became illegal to wish someone Merry Christmas, and it was frowned upon to say, 'God bless you,' when somebody sneezed. If you say the name, Jesus, and someone gets offended, you could go to jail. Unless of course you were using it as a curse word. Atheistic policymakers were drooling; they were finally getting the chance to silence Christians everywhere; this time it was legal."

"Now it's gone beyond just religion," Jacob shook his head. "Since I got out of lock up, I'm afraid to send an undercooked steak back for fear of offending the cook. You know how my mouth used to work. I thought it, I said it. I'm amazed I didn't end up in jail sooner than I did." Jacob paused a moment, reflecting on how much life has changed. He sighed, "the good ole Anti Dehumanization Act. I still can't believe that it is illegal to speak against anyone holding an elected position. I mean, c'mon, isn't that part of what we fought the American Revolution over?"

"So much for, 'I may not agree with what you say, but I'll defend to the death your right to say it,'" Eric concurred. "From the time the judgement was issued I was a marked man. Not long after I relocated here, I got a letter in the mail. It didn't have a return address, but it was postmarked Atlanta. It simply said, 'I've got my eye on you.'"

"Edwards?" Jacob asked.

"He wasn't an Official back then," Eric said. "But he was the assistant district attorney in charge of building the case against me. I didn't know him before the charges were filed. I'd never heard of him. But he was quick to make himself known. Edwards made my life a living hell, and it wasn't even about the case, I don't think. It was something more, I don't know, personal. He wasn't happy about losing the criminal case. The judge said there was no precedent to award in their favor. Edwards was the one who encouraged Mathis to file the civil suit, which as you just read, they won. Edwards even stepped down as Atlanta ADA to serve as a Federal prosecuting attorney. His protégé Philip Duncan took over as ADA to keep an eye on me until the Federal law was passed.

"Edwards was the one who lobbied with the Governor to pass the law and set a precedent, using our case as an example. But he wasn't satisfied with state law. He lobbied for a federal law patterned after the new Georgia statute. He was successful. As a reward, he was selected to head the congressional task force to enforce the new laws. Of course, by then, I was long gone. Not even Philip Duncan knew where I was. So, Edwards began his search for me. When he found me, he sent the letter and waited until the opportunity was right. He planted a spy in my church. The rest is history."

"Wow," was all Jacob could say.

"Edwards assigned himself jurisdiction over the Texas-New Mexico region. I'm not sure what I ever did to him, and maybe I'm just being paranoid, but I think it's a personal vendetta against me. I heard he's training more Officials."

"I think I know who may be one of them," Jacob said, sadness tinging his words.

"Really? How can you be sure?"

"When I was released, a friend, Jesse, came to visit me. He took me to lunch and asked about my stay in prison. We talked about the past, and I apologized to him and about the things I had put him through, and I even asked him about his faith. I didn't give it much thought at the time, but he was driving a brand-new black Denali.

"Later, I talked to Renae. She said that she thought I was dead, that she had received a phone call saying I was killed trying to escape. She told me Jesse comforted her through her grief and now they are together. Coincidence? I don't think so.

"Add insult to injury, I'm pretty sure I'm being followed. By a black Denali. I'm afraid my closest friend is an Official in training."

"Wow. I'm sorry, Jacob. I know it hurts when the ones closest to you betray you. Just know that you have friends here."

Their conversation was interrupted by the sound of footsteps approaching the inner door. It creaked open, and Roger poked his head through the opening. "Howdy, Pastor," he said as he sauntered into the room. "How ya doing, Jacob?"

"Welcome to the party," Eric said as he grabbed him in a hug. "Glad you could make it. Will and Frank will be here shortly."

"Yeah, I saw Frank's car up the road. He was doing the normal routine."

"Normal routine?" Jacob asked.

"Checking for a tail," Roger explained. "They don't always drive Denali's. They only drive those when they want you to see them, so you know you're being watched. They're trying to put the fear of God into you. Or I guess in this case, the fear of not-God. When they want to stay hidden, they drive a regular vehicle to blend in. I don't worry when I see a Denali. I worry when I don't."

"Roger was with me in Atlanta. Both him and Jessica," Eric explained. "The parts store is part of the network we have. William is the outside source we use to communicate with others across the country. You think what we went through is bad, you should see it in Atlanta, where the laws have been enforced for a while. Officials don't allow the media to show any of it. And the media doesn't put up a fight. If they do, they are subject to the same penalties as those who 'broke the law' that they were trying to record.

"As soon as Edwards obtained his position, he came back to Atlanta, but I had already brought my family here. Others like Roger and Jessica followed me. Will took me in soon after I relocated to Texas. I tried to keep them away, but their devotion was solid, and to be honest, much needed."

"Now there is an underground. Many others across the country, just like us, keeping God's word alive," Roger said.

"This Anti Dehumanization movement is escalating more rapidly than anyone expected," Eric said. "You'd think the U.S., the last protector of freedom, would be okay, but give it a bit. Soon you'll see how far these laws will go. I've already been imprisoned for addressing the sinfulness of man. And you were arrested for raising your voice to an Official. I suspect things will get much, much worse before they get better."

The door creaked open, and Frank and William entered the room.

"Gentleman," Eric chimed. "So glad you could make it. You all know Jacob?"

They all greet each other with familial smiles and hugs. Jacob watched them with a certain level of envy, if he was being honest with himself. Each man had an air about him that was unlike anything Jacob had experienced before. They seemed to fit together, a band of brothers where everyone was equal. But each had a unique quality. Eric had his boldness; Will his loving burliness. Roger was small and quiet, unassuming but completely self-assured. And Frank—well, Frank was country to the bone: Six-foot-five, hat and boots with a tweed blazer. Frank was a bear of a man. Where Jacob stood in their eyes was anyone's guess. But one thing he was sure of, he was welcome.

"Sorry we're late, Pastor," Will stated. "I had issues leaving the shop today. The gray Denali was driving around the area, more than likely trying to find my shop. I'm thinkin' maybe he tailed Jacob up there yesterday."

"Yeah, I'm sorry about that," Jacob apologized.

"No worries. How could you have known?"

"Just as long as we do our best not to get our tails followed here," Frank said with a wink.

"Yes, Frank, nice piece of driving. Saw you on my way here," said Roger.

Frank nodded, tipping his hat.

"Let's go ahead and get started."

Eric introduced Jacob to the group, giving his back story and how he came to Christ in prison. They discussed the stories coming out of Atlanta, Des Moines, and Boulder, each one more horrifying than the previous—rumors of imprisonments and beatings, even one execution. The Officials appointed to the area were given all-means-necessary authority. Some took it to the extreme.

They also discussed stories of the Word of God still being preached despite the laws, of small groups of people meeting on the outskirts of smaller towns, like Carrelton. As Eric said, *there more of us than you know.*

Finally, Eric spoke of plans for a church service. The where and when would be determined later. They all knew it would be difficult. They had a hard enough time walking from their car to their house without an Official knowing about it. But the Officials couldn't be everywhere at once. Their determination outweighed their fears.

Everyone agreed it would need to have a small-town, Sunday night church feel to it; a brief time of worship followed by a message from God's Word. Jacob was excited at the thought. He actually couldn't remember ever attending a church service he *wanted* to be at. Eric asked Frank to close their meeting with a prayer. The men held hands and bowed their heads.

Soon they were on their way through the darkened path to the parking lot. Clouds obscured the moon, but they knew the way by heart. They walked silently, single file through the maze of brush and debris, each car peeling off in a different direction out of the lot.

"You have a great bunch of guys, Eric," Jacob commended once they were on the road.

"I know. I trust those men. Just like I trust you." Eric drove in darkness until he reached the highway. He flicked on his lights, he headed toward Jacobs apartment. "If you need anything, you can go to any of them. They will treat you well. You can trust them."

"How often do you have these meetings?"

"Not as often as we'd like. We never set a time or place in advance—you never know who might be listening. When the time comes you'll be contacted, much like you were contacted by me through Will at his shop. Until then, we live out our lives as normal."

"Normal. What's normal anymore?" Jacob asked.

"I will find out tomorrow," Eric replied with a chuckle. "Maybe Margaret needs a good busboy."

"I never had the chance to thank you."

"For what?"

"For your kindness and patience. I'm pretty sure I came across rude or insensitive to you at the beginning. I apologize. Your friendship helped me get through the time I spent in jail."

"I'm just the man God made me. I am glad it was a blessing to you. I pray that you allow that to be a blessing to others."

"I still don't know what to do about Renae and Michael. I don't know if her heart still holds a place for me or if the pain I caused was too much. I mean, she thought I was dead. She shut that part of her life off. Now that I am back, does it mean we still have a chance? I think what scares me most is thinking about her being with Jesse. Maybe if it was the old Jesse I might be okay with it. At least I could deal with it. But if Jesse really is an Official, and she with him, is she *with* him? Or is she still in the dark about what he's become? Eric, I don't know what to do."

"Wish I had an easy answer for you, my friend. Sometimes all you can do is pray for guidance. God will show you where to go, what to do, what to say."

Eric stopped in from of Jacob's apartment. As Jacob opened the door he said, "Be careful out there. We'll meet again soon, after things have calmed down a bit. Now that we're both back out on the street, you can be sure the Officials are on heightened alert. They'd love nothing more than to lock us all up and throw away the keys. Do your best to not give them that opportunity."

"Good night, my friend," Jacob said. "Thanks again." Jacob

watched until the taillights of Eric's car faded from sight, then he pulled the key from his pocket and unlocked his front door. It was definitely time to call it a day.

‖‖‖ ‖‖‖ ‖‖‖

There was an unusual number of cars in front of Mills Motors for a Saturday evening—10, not counting the vehicles that were being repaired or serviced. The shop bay was empty. A couple of dozen fold-out chairs assumed the place of toolboxes. People from around town filtered in; a couple of servers from Dunham's, a clerk from the grocery store, and Aaron, one of the cooks from Maggie's. There were a number that Jacob didn't recognize, perhaps members of Eric's church up in Polk? It made him nervous to see so many unfamiliar faces, but the men he'd already met were there. That helped.

The first service of the Carrelton Underground Church got underway. Eric thanked everyone for coming. He acknowledge the risk they were taking, and was humbled by it. Frank picked up a guitar and began to play. *He's good*, Jacob thought. *Very good*. Voices mingled with Frank's guitar as the familiar tunes of "Amazing Grace" and "How Great Thou Art" filled the room. Jessica stood and sang a song he was unfamiliar with, but instantly fell in love with.

"I come to the garden alone…" she crooned.

"She has some amazing pipes," Jacob whispered to the gentleman next to him.

"Amen," he agreed.

Once the singing ended, Eric rose and told the story of his time in prison, of meeting Jacob and the bond they shared, always giving credit to the power of God for getting them both through it. "I don't know what would have happened to me if it weren't for our new brother Jacob. Shortly before we met, I heard a man being tortured and killed, and I was unable to do anything to stop it or to even alleviate that man's pain. It broke me; I'll be honest. I didn't want to go on. Why would God allow me to listen to a defenseless man suffer and die? Where was the compassion in that? Where was God's love? I'm sure many of you have experienced times when you felt like God was nowhere to be found.

"Many of you were part of Polk. Perhaps you may have felt defenseless as I was taken away. I'm asking you not to carry that burden. What man meant for destruction, God meant for his glory. There is a purpose for everything; I believe that! While I am not sure why I had to experience Kenneth's death, I know now that my purpose was to help save someone I would most likely have not met otherwise—Jacob Andrews. Jacob saved me."

Jacob's head shot up and he stared slack-jawed at the pastor.

"Yes, he was a bit abrasive at first." Eric grinned as he glanced at Jacob. "He had no filter when it came to saying what he thought; no control over the words he spoke. But he saved me. Jacob once asked me why I didn't talk to him about God sooner than I did. I'm pretty sure I gave him a spiritually satisfying answer about waiting for the right time, and the unction of the Holy Spirit. But you want to know the real answer? It was because I doubted. I was on the verge of losing my faith. I'd seen too many men come and go in that prison, most of the time without any indication they were gone, other than the silence when I would call to them. That last man, his name was Kenneth, that was the final straw for me. They wanted to break me—and for a moment they did.

"It was the 'Every failure is the beginning of a new adventure' sermon I preached before I was arrested; the same sermon I preached in Atlanta that set this whole thing in motion. It was me saying those words to you Jacob, that brought me back. A reminder that all of this *is* the new adventure—dark and gloomy as it may be. We may have to stumble our way through the night to meet together. But in the end, it is a grand adventure if each step brings us closer to Christ.

"Each of you has stood with me, fully knowing you could be dragged down as well. Roger and Jessica stood by my side when the cameras were rolling. Through the name calling, the finger pointing, and the hate that was spewed at us. They know it, all too well.

"Will, you took me and my family in when we moved to Texas. You felt the calling to assist, and for that, I am forever grateful. You helped us settle into Polk and to find a place to live." Eric's eyes filled with tears and his voice quavered. "You were there when… When Kathy and the girls went to be with the Lord on that cold and rainy day. You were a Godsend. Thank you.

"Many others felt the call to pursue the freedom we knew to be true. To be in a position to help our brothers and sisters across the country who are facing the same struggles. Without you, this church wouldn't exist. *You* are the church. And God working in you is how we survive. We must pull together like never before. Officials are ever-watching. Now, the biggest test awaits. And we will pass the test, together.

"We will pass because we all have gifts we need to serve our Lord. Will, yours is hospitality. You know how to make people feel welcome. Roger, you and Jessica know service and how to meet people's needs. Frank, you have a mind for business. I'm not sure that's listed in the Bible as a spiritual gift, but I can assure you, my friend, it truly is. Without level heads and smart minds, those of us who are weaker could not accomplish the goal set before us. We need your wise counsel.

"Me, I'm just a man with a microphone. I'm the Lord's tool, a voice that his Spirit speaks through. But I lack boldness. The boldness that Jacob possesses is light-years beyond anything I would dare to dream of having within myself. These brothers and sisters are the core of this church. You know that any of them would sacrifice themselves for any of you.

"I implore you, use your gifts together. They complement each other, and are not nearly effective when used alone. So, discover your gift. Seek God, and he will show you, then use that gift boldly. Ask God to build up the desire to use it. In 2 Timothy 1:6 Paul writes, '*Therefore, I remind you to stir up the gift of God that is in you.*' Seek it, find it, use it. Stir it up for His glory. Let's pray."

As Jacob listened to Eric's prayer, he recalled the dark days in prison hearing Eric's muffled, whispered prayers each night. Tonight his voice carried the same cadence those prayers did. It was soothing. It drew you in, made you feel the passion behind the words. You could tell Eric truly believed what he was saying. He fully believed that Christ was in all that was going on. He believed if the church were willing to commit as he had, there would be nothing to stop them.

Jacob shook hands or embraced nearly everyone there. But compared to Will, all hugs paled in comparison. He enjoyed himself. He felt part of a family. He hadn't felt that sense of belonging in quite a while. Even with Renae and Michael, he'd always felt disconnected. Through the process of missed opportunities, he'd taken those closest to him for granted. Now, they were gone.

But this new group didn't know about his past. All they saw was the new him; the new him that had an encounter with God. That made him happy. He prayed that when those who knew him before, saw him now, they would recognize the change, that it would be a great example of how God can work in the life of anyone—there is no one too far gone.

As the crowd was dispersed into the darkness of night, Eric approached Jacob. "Well, I'm relieved."

"What about?"

"That was my first time speaking to a crowd in over a year. I wondered if I still had it in me." Eric then looked at Jacob intently. "I meant what I said. If it weren't for you being in that cell next to me, I don't know where I would be right now. Emotionally or physically. Thank you."

"I should be the one thanking you. You allowed God to speak through you to help save me. If it weren't for you, I wouldn't be here right now. I'd either be stuck back in the miserable life I had before, or I'd be dead."

"Let's say we saved each other," Eric laughed.

"Agreed." Jacob extended his hand.

"You're not getting off that easy." Eric pulls him in for a hug. "Do you work tomorrow?"

"Don't I always?"

"I guess you do." He leaned in and whispered, "Would you be able to meet me tomorrow evening at the storm shelter? I want to discuss something with you. Can't do it here."

"Sure, I get off at 5 p.m."

Will approached. "Pastor, can I speak to you? How are you, Jacob?"

"I'm good. I'll let you two talk." Jacob said, excusing himself.

"No, I would like you to hear this too, Jacob." Will looked concerned. "I'm scared Pastor. I know they're searching for me up in New B. It's only a matter of time now until they find my shop. I keep seeing that silver Denali—Edwards' deputies I suppose. They have increased their patrols. Now, I fear for all of us. He's out for revenge, and I think I am next on his list."

"Will, we're in this together. Don't for on minute think that I have forgotten what you did for me after Atlanta. I have told Jacob all about the sacrifices you made for my family and me. Even though he may be new to our circle, he is willing to give just as much as any of us would. Don't be afraid. God has a plan in all of this; He is in control. If you do feel overwhelmed, we are just a phone call away."

Will let out a sigh: his body lifted and then deflated, but he managed to smile. "Thank you, Pastor, that helps. Thank you, Jacob. I have a good feeling about you." He gave Jacob another patented Will-hug. "See you guys next meeting. God Bless."

They both watched him walk out the door. "Will is an amazing man of God. He was there for me in my struggle. We need to be there for him in his. Keep your phone close at hand. He seems to have taken a liking to you. I would not be surprised if he calls you before he calls me."

Jacob was nervous for Will. He had yet to witness fear in a Christian. Both Eric and Will showed such strength. It made him feel safe. It made his want to grow that strong himself. To see someone he respected confess fear shook him. "Eric, if someone like Will is afraid, even at his level of faith, what hope is there for me?"

"It proves we are all human, Jacob," Eric said. "If we were

perfect we wouldn't need faith. Faith is acting when you can't see the end. It's taking a breath and moving forward not knowing what is next. We are all doing that right now. And Satan hates it because we are succeeding. It's no wonder his attacks on the faithful ones are increasing. He hopes to take us all down by taking one of us down. Sometimes that's all it takes. But no matter what happens, we need to stay the course.

"The man in Atlanta was just the tipping point. Why it happened within the church I pastored is beyond me. Why I was chosen by God to bear this burden remains to be seen. Regardless, the fight is real. Jacob, we are on the verge of it being illegal to be a Christian. Our mere presence will be offensive. I for one, cannot remain silent. How can we win souls if we do not preach Christ? It's up to us now. My calling has directed me here. I am confident that you are part of this calling. I pray you feel it too."

Jacob knew what Eric was talking about. Although he was new to all of this, he felt an urge to pass on what he has been taught. He wanted to help others see what he has seen. He was ready for the fight.

"I'm ready, Eric. Something is coming; something big. I don't know if being shoved into the deep end is from the Holy Spirit or the devil. But whoever, or whatever, is orchestrating it, I say, bring it on!"

Things returned to normal for the next few days. Jacob developed a morning routine—waking up to a cup of coffee and an open Bible. He loved reading stories about Jesus and his followers, but he felt a special kinship to Paul. Paul went from condemning to encouraging people. That's what he wanted to do. He loved his morning *devotional* time, as Eric called it. Whatever it was, he couldn't get enough.

After an hour of study, he worked his shift at the hardware store. No deliveries to Will's shop, but a couple to Mills Motors. He felt like part of a secret society when he walked in. Jessica would give him a hearty greeting and a wink. Roger would come out, and they would talk shop for a bit, and an occasional word about a meeting that was coming soon. Eric was making plans for a regular service, perhaps in the storm shelter. He was always excited to visit his new friends—brothers and sisters in Christ, as Eric would put it.

His days ended back at his apartment with a Hungry Man and a Diet Dr. Pepper. He often fell asleep thinking of Renae and Michael. He missed them. Sometimes Jacob recalled the nights spent in his cell, anticipating getting out and reuniting with them. If *wishes were wings a frog wouldn't bump his butt*, his mother used to say. He had caused Renae to leave. He must live with that.

Jacob was getting ready to call Renae, to have another

one-sided conversation about the possibility of seeing Michael, when his phone rang. He glanced at caller ID, then pressed the answer button. "Hey Will, what's up?"

"Jacob! Jacob, he's here. He found me! Oh no! I gotta go." The line went dead.

"Will?" Jacob was standing now, heart-pounding "Will?"

Jacob scrolled through his contacts and dialed Eric. A half-awake voice stammered, "Jacob? It's late; what's wrong?"

"It's Will." Jacob didn't know where to begin. He felt like he was blathering. "Something's wrong. He called me and said that 'he is here.' Then the line went dead. I think Edwards found him."

"I'll be there in 15 minutes."

Jacob paced for a few moments, then could stand it no longer. He went outside to wait, locking the door to the apartment behind him. Something was wrong. Something was very wrong. The next fifteen minutes seemed like an eternity. He neck tensed and his breathing started coming in shallow gulps. For a moment he thought he might pass out, so he sat down on the curb, put his head between his knees, and forced his breathing to slow. He closed his eyes and began to pray. What he wanted to say was, "Lord, I don't know what's going on. I find myself afraid for Will. I pray that you are with him and protect him. I know your will will be accomplished no matter what happens. I just ask that you save my friend." What actually came out sounded more like, "Oh God, oh God, o God, oh God!"

Eric's big Buick squealed to a stop, and Eric hopped out. "Jacob, you okay?"

Jacob stood and opened the door to get in. "I'm a little overwhelmed."

"I know how you feel," Eric said. "I'll get us there as quick as I can."

The drive from Carrelton to New Braunfels normally took an hour and a half in light traffic. It was after midnight. What little traffic that was on the road offered little impediment. Eric exceeded every speed limit sign on the quiet drive up Interstate 35. As they approached their exit, they could see two emergency vehicles driving on the frontage road turning down Highway 46.

Jacob's eyes followed their path. "Oh no, Will!" The darkness couldn't hide the black billows of smoke rising in the distance, and an ominous orange glow danced with the flashing red lights against them.

"Hold on," Eric said as he floored it.

They followed the direction of the two vehicles and came upon police and sheriff vehicles that blocked the road. They pulled over and got out. "Officer, what's going on?" Eric asked.

"A business fire," said the officer. He was tall and thin and held a Mag-light.

"What business?" Jacob asked.

"Not sure. This isn't my part of town," the officer said as he waved another emergency vehicle through.

"Can we go up there? Our friend's business is up there. We'd like to see if he is okay." Eric asked.

"Too dangerous, sorry."

Jacob looked at the officer's badge, "Officer Sanders, please? He's my brother," said Jacob.

The officer looked at them, then looked around and nodded his head. Eric and Jacob ducked under the caution tape and sprinted towards Will's shop.

"Be careful," shouted Sanders.

Fire trucks lined the road. An EMS vehicle was parked just inside the entrance. Jacob saw the gate, the five-barred gate, lying on its side, smashed to pieces. Jacob stopped. "I wonder if the firefighters did that getting in here—or someone else?"

"My bet is someone else," Eric said, his mouth in a thin, grim line.

Will's shop was engulfed in flames. Firefighters were making no progress on putting it out. The best they could hope to do was keep it from spreading. "Let it burn itself out," someone shouted. "It's contained. Monitor the surrounding area for spreading."

Jacob saw a fireman who appeared to be in charge and shouted, "That's my friend's shop. Save it!"

"How did you get in here?" The fire captain pointed back toward the highway. "You need to get out of here; it's too dangerous. Anyway, we can't save it. It's too far gone. There is way too much flammable material inside, and this truck does not have Class B foam. Plain water on it would only spread the flames."

"Where's the owner?" Eric asked.

"I don't know. Haven't seen him."

"Have you tried his home up the ranch road?" Eric suggested.

"Yes, we looked there. A work truck was there, but no one answered."

"Eric, you don't think—"

Eric looked at the fire. "I don't know what to think, Jacob. I just don't know."

Jacob saw the look on Eric's face. It showed the same thing he was feeling. Their friend was gone. "Edwards must have found him."

The flash of the lights and the smell of the smoke made

Jacob dizzy. The confusion left him disoriented. The fire trucks, water trucks feeding into them. EMS vehicle behind the entrance, the inferno in front of him. It was surreal. He felt as if he were watching a movie—present but disconnected; like what he was seeing was through some else's eyes. All sound was drowned out by the drumming of his heavy heart in his ears.

"What now?" Jacob asked.

"We wait," Eric said. "We need to know for sure."

A fire truck with *San Antonio FD* on the door pulled through the gate. One of the men shouted to the Captain, "Class B is here!"

"Well, it's about time!" The captain waved a couple of his men toward the truck, and before it even came to a complete stop, men were pulling hoses off and connecting the feeder lines to the Jones Water Service truck.

"Go! Go! Go!" another fireman shouted as three others ran to the fire. Opening the line, they were at last making progress at extinguishing the flames.

An hour later the flames were gone All that remained were small patches of smoldering wood. The captain was walking through a patch of rubble when one of his men called out, "Cap! Over here. One body."

The lump growing in Jacob's throat almost choked him. He felt nauseated as a two-member EMS crew rolled a stretcher through a maze of charred material. They emerged several minutes later with a long, black bag on top of the stretcher. There was little doubt as to who it contained.

Tears mingled with black soot left gray streaks down Jacob's cheeks. The bile in this throat took over and he rushed to some nearby bushes and emptied his stomach. Hunched over, trying to regain his equilibrium, he jumped when he felt a hand on his back.

"You okay?" Eric asked.

"No," Jacob stammered. "I'm not okay. I'm not sure I'm ever going to be okay after this. I just can't believe this is happening. Will was a good guy. Why?"

"I don't know why, brother," Eric said as the fire captain approached carrying a couple bottles of water.

"Did you know the owner?" he asked.

"Yes, sir," Eric said. "He was a close friend."

"I'm sorry for your loss," the man said. "I'm Captain James Dell. Is there anything you can tell me about what may have happened?"

Jacob started to tell Captain James Dell exactly what happened, but a sharp look from Eric silenced him. "No Captain, we have no clue. We were driving back from Austin and saw the glow of the fire," said Eric. "We knew our friend's shop was down this way, so we stopped."

"Okay. Thank you," he said replacing this hardhat, turned, and walked away. Then he stopped and came back. "Again, I'm sorry for your loss. Before you leave, Sergeant Powell over there may want to speak with you."

"Certainly, Captain." Eric shook hands with him.

"I thought lying was a sin," Jacob said as the captain returned to his duties.

"There are lies, and there are lies," Eric said. "What he doesn't need to know, he doesn't need to know. Bottom line, we don't know who is for us or who is against us."

"You don't think—"

"I don't know what to think, but it's better to exhibit caution, than to give someone the benefit of the doubt and be wrong."

"You think Edwards is behind this?"

"We both know he was," Eric said, a hard edge to his reply. He took one last look at what was left of Will's shop. "We should go now."

On their way out they gave their names and numbers to Sergeant Powell and left.

The ride back felt far longer than the ride up. Silence filled the space between the friends. Jacob had only known Will for a little over a month, but the pain was like when his parents died. There was a spiritual connection that went beyond time. He could only imagine what Eric was going through.

They made their way through south San Antonio. The highway was unnaturally empty. The streetlights glowed without a hint of mourning or of the tragedy they had just experienced.

"How are you holding up, Eric?"

Eric gripped the steering wheel tighter and kept his eyes forward on the road. "I don't know. I think I should be feeling sadness over Wills death. I think I should feel anger at Edwards and his crew. I think I should feel a lot of things. But right now, I'm not sure I feel anything.. Maybe it's too soon; maybe it's all happening too fast."

"I guess I'm just confused by all of it," Jacob said. "I mean, why? I'm not questioning God or anything, I'm wondering what Edwards had to gain by killing Will? Will was no threat to him."

"I don't think Edwards felt threatened. I think he wanted revenge. Against me. For Atlanta."

"But he won his case."

"For people like Edwards, winning isn't enough. Edwards views Christians as the enemy, an enemy to be utterly crushed, ground into the dirt, and wiped off your heal before you walk into the house. I think he was using Will to hurt me. He'll use others too, I have no doubt."

"Jesse," Jacob spat. "I should have known something was up. It was too convenient that he would visit me on the day I was released. How could he have known, unless someone told him? Unless someone sent him? When I asked him about his new job, he changed the subject. I knew something was off, but I never expected this."

"It's in the past now. We move on. Edwards wants us to give up. It's personal to him."

Jacob stared at the white lines on the road, rushing past. "It's personal to me too."

Eric nodded.

The sun was peeking over the horizon when Eric dropped Jacob off. "You work today?"

"Unfortunately," Jacob said, exiting the car. "But I don't go in until 10. I can grab a few hours of sleep."

"Be careful. Edwards will be waiting to see our reaction. I'll talk with Roger and Frank, let them know what happened before it hits the headlines. I'll get a message to you when we will meet again. For now, I think the best reaction, is no reaction. So, just go about your normal routine, as if last night didn't happen."

"Like nothing happened. Right." Jacob blew out a breath and squinted at the rising sun. "I'm sorry Eric. I know you two were close. If you need to talk, I'm here."

"Thank you, brother," Eric said. "That means a lot."

Jacob watched as he drove away, scanning the area for signs of unwelcome company. Sunlight spilled over the rooftops onto the parking lot. No sign of any Denalis—black, white.

or silver. A shiver ran down his spine as he recalled Roger's comment, *They don't always drive Denalis. When they want to stay hidden, they drive a regular vehicle to blend in.* He looked around for anything out of the ordinary, then quickly entered his apartment, locked the door behind him, and crashed on his bed, exhausted.

He slept until the phone in his pocket buzzed him awake. Bright daylight shone through the blinds. He looked at the clock: 10:45. He fumbled for his cellphone.

"Hello," he mumbled.

"You planning to show up today, Jacob?"

It was his boss, Stan, and he was not happy.

"Yes. I'm sorry, Stan. Had an emergency last night. On my way."

He punched the off button, splashed some water on his face, changed clothes and headed to work. The events of the previous night weighed heavy on his heart. He wanted answers. He needed closure. And both could be found in one man—Jesse. He didn't know where Jesse lived. He didn't know his phone number. But he did know a common source—Renae.

Jacob's face turned to stone. He might just have to pay her a visit.

ꟼꟼꟼ

||||| ||||| |||||

Wednesday and Thursday were Jacob's days off. He hadn't heard from Eric since *the event*. He figured Eric was sticking to the plan of laying low. *Give Edwards the impression we had indeed given up.* The news of the fire at Will's shop was a blip in the local paper. The fire was labeled as suspicious, but no evidence was found linking anyone to the it and no motive was evident. The photo accompanying the article showed nothing but a large, charred pile of rubble.

Jacob was on his way to the grocery store to pick up a fresh supply of Hungry Mans when he spotted the Black Denali again. It disappeared so quickly that he thought he might have been imagining it. But he caught a glimpse of it again when he stopped for gas. His cell rang halfway through his fill-up.

"Hey Eric," Jacob said. "How are things?"

"I think our friends are back," Eric stated.

"Yep. I'm looking at one now," Jacob concurred. "Where are you?"

"Just outside of town. I went up to New Braunfels. Will's sister came down from Minnesota to finalize everything. Their parents are gone, and it was just the two of them. I was assisting and consoling. I was leaving town when I first saw him. He's been about a quarter mile behind me ever since."

"Any plans?" Jacob asked.

"Not at this point. We'll meet this weekend sometime. I've

already talked to Frank and Roger. Both are open to the idea, just needed to confirm with you."

"I'm off the next couple of days, but I work this weekend. I am free in the evenings, though."

"Friday then. Same time and place?"

"Sounds like a plan. See you then."

Jacob hung up and just stared at the truck. It just sat there, like a vulture, watching. Anger welled up inside. *It's time to do something, but approaching the Denali didn't work last time. No reason it would now.* The automatic pump clicked off, and he returned the nozzle to the dispenser. *I'll call Renae. Maybe she would be willing to set up a meeting with Jesse.*

Jacob returned home, put away his meal rations, and settled on the couch. He laid his phone on the table, pondering making the call to Renae. *What if she knows about Jesse?* The thought made him sick, and more than a little angry. *That's not the woman I fell in love with. She has to be in the dark. Only one way to find out.*

Jacob snatched up the phone and dialed before he lost his nerve.

One ring. Two rings. Three—"What is it, Jacob?" Renae's irritation radiated over the line.

"Hey, Renae. How are you doing?"

"I'm fine Jacob. What do you want? I haven't changed my mind about Michael, so unless there's something else you need to talk about, I'm busy."

"Yes, I have a reason," Jacob reasoned, calmly. "I need to talk to you, and it isn't about Michael, and yes, it is important, but it's not something we can talk about over the phone. I need to see you. Face to face."

"What is so important?"

"I'll tell you when we meet. Just tell me when and where."

"I don't know Jacob. I'd have to find a sitter for Michael. Let me talk to Jesse and—"

"No!" Jacob's response was harsher than he'd intended. He tried again. "No, Renae. Please, it's important you don't mention this to him."

"Why?"

"I will explain everything, I promise. Please just trust me this one time, and don't say anything to Jesse."

"Alright. I guess I can meet you tomorrow during my lunch break. Jesse is going to Austin for some distributor meeting. He'll be gone all day. Where do you want to meet?"

"Maggie's is as good of a place as any. What time?"

"Twelve-thirty. Maggie's is fine. I'll see you then, Jake. And Jake? This better be important."

"It is. Thank y—"

The call disconnected before he could complete his sentence. Jacob stared at the phone, feeling lost and more alone than he had since getting out of lock-up. Hearing Renae's voice was balm to his soul and a knife in his ribs. He wasn't sure which hurt worse.

Wonder if the Bible has anything to say about situations like this? He grabbed Renae's Bible from the table and flipped through it to the story about Paul going into Jerusalem to meet with the apostles for the first time. He'd read it multiple times since coming to faith, and it was one of his favorites. He knew it almost by heart. The apostles were afraid. They didn't believe his conversion was real. After all, this same guy had been hunting down Christians, putting them in chains, and even putting some to death. Now he was preaching Jesus was the Messiah?

Much like Paul didn't know what to expect when he saw Peter, he didn't know what to expect from Renae. Was she merely curious about what was so important, or was she a pawn in a bigger picture, or worse, was she working with Jesse and Edwards? A brief prayer confirmed his conclusion: He needed to call for back up. He grabbed his phone and dialed.

"Hey Eric, are you busy tomorrow?"

†††

Jacob was restless. He'd had a multitude of imaginary conversations with Renae on his way to Maggie's. None of them ended well. He sat in the booth sipping his third cup of coffee, wondering whether she would even show up, or if she had confided their clandestine meeting to Jesse. He chose the same booth he'd used for their last meeting, the one that gave the best view of the parking area. He arrived a couple of hours early, just to scout the area for anything out of the ordinary.

"You get stood up sweetie?" Margaret asked. The pencil which was normally behind her ear was now in her hand waiting to write down his order in shorthand that only a pharmacist or a short-order cook could decipher.

"I'm a bit early," Jacob replied. "I could do with a warm-up"

"It's the best coffee in town," Margaret said as she poured.

"You got that right. I'll order in a few minutes, whether my friend shows up or not."

Jacob sweetened his coffee and took slow sip. Renae pulled up. And she was alone. At least so it seemed. No Black Denali in sight. *When they want to stay hidden, they drive a regular vehicle to blend in.* Jacob scanned the parking lot, but didn't see anything out of the ordinary.

Renae, looking gorgeous as usual, seemed to glide through the doors and into the diner. She saw him right away and made her way to the booth.

"Hello, Renae. How are you?" Jacob stood until she was seated.

"Hello, Jacob." Renae looked at her watch. "Let's make this quick. I only have an hour, and I spent 15 minutes driving here."

"You want anything?" Jacob said, pointing to a menu. "My treat?"

"No, I am fine."

Jacob waved at Margaret and said, "I'll have the bacon cheeseburger plate, well done. Just water for my friend."

Margaret gave him a thumb's up.

He took a breath and looked straight into those emerald eyes that had beguiled him so many times when he was a younger man. He expected to see coldness, bitterness. He saw neither. What he saw was hurt, unspoken pain, and something he couldn't put his finger on. Longing, perhaps? It caught him off guard. He stared for a moment too long because she snapped her fingers in front of her face and said, "What?"

Jacob immediately returned back to his purpose. "What type of work does Jesse do?" There was no subtle way of asking. May as well get to the point.

"He works for an IT center based out of Austin," she said.

"Are you sure about that?"

"Jacob, this is ridiculous. Of course I'm sure. It's all highly confidential, and he can't talk much about it without breaking like a hundred federal laws. He doesn't tell and I don't ask."

"Are you familiar with the Anti-Dehumanization Act?" Jacob asked.

"Yes, we just had a training module on it not too long ago. Why? What does this have to do with—"

"So, you understand the restrictions it puts on what you can and cannot say to people?"

"Yes. Of course. We just have to watch what products we attempt to sell customers so they don't take offense. Sales have gone down. No one is meeting their goals, and we didn't make our bonus payout last quarter. The tellers are afraid to ask how a customer's day is going, much less ask them to sit with a banker to see how we can help them. It's made my job a lot harder. What does all this have to do with Jesse?"

"While I was—away, I met a man, a pastor of a church up in Polk. You want to know why he was in prison? He was arrested for preaching a sermon saying people need Jesus. He was imprisoned for a year."

"And this has *what* to do with me?"

"You know about the federal police officers, called Officials, who monitor the enforcement of the Anti-Dehumanization Act?"

"Like the one who took you away?" A sudden look of confusion crossed her face. "The one who called me and told me you were dead."

"Yes. That Official's name is Edwards. He has jurisdiction in our area, and he takes his job very seriously. He has deputies working under him; low level officers who monitor the compliance with the law in public places, like banks… and churches. They try to find people using so-called offensive speech."

The wrinkle between her eyes became more pronounced as the pieces started falling into place. "You think Jesse is one of them?"

"I know he is. I'm sorry Renae, but Jesse is part of it."

"Even if he is, what's wrong with working in law enforcement?"

"Law enforcement is not the problem. It's the law itself, and how it is affecting every freedom this country was built on. You know how this whole thing started as a result of that church in Georgia, right?"

"Yes, it was part of the module."

"Official Edwards was chief prosecutor. Now he's turned into chief persecutor, and there's a big difference in those two nouns. The pastor of that church fled from Georgia to Texas, to escape his persecution. But Edwards followed him to the state, hell-bent on exacting his revenge, not only on that pastor, but on every person who proclaims the name of Jesus Christ."

"That's absurd. Even if that's true, why should you care? You're not a Christian."

Jacob sat silent, and just stared at her.

"You're not a Christian. Are you?"

"Yes, I am," Jacob said with a hint of a smile. "The man in the cell adjacent to mine was a pastor. Through our conversations, he led me to the Lord. But I can tell you about that another time. What is important right now is that Eric was that Atlanta pastor.

"Renae, Officials are well paid. They have a virtually unlimited expense account, they operate on a level that is above the law. They can't be prosecuted. They can't even be accused of overstepping the law, because the law doesn't apply to them. You know what I am saying is true. You have concerns about what Jesse does."

"Jesse works for an IT company—

"In Austin. All very hush, hush. I know. You told me. But you don't believe it. One last thing. Officials are provided with a company car. Would you like to guess what kind?"

"No."

"GMC Denali."

Renae dropped her eyes and shook her head, but the denial was gone. She looked defeated. It broke Jacob's heart, but he knew he couldn't stop now.

"I'm so sorry to have to be the one to tell you this, but it must be said."

"There's more?"

"I am afraid there is." Jacob started. "The fire in New Braunfels, the one that killed that man? That was set by Officials. I cannot say Jesse was directly involved because I have no proof. But the people he works for are most definitely responsible."

"Oh God," Renae said. She closed her eyes and held out her hand, not wanting to hear any more.

"The attacks against innocent people are growing worse by the week. Home are being searched without warrants. Housewives and grandmothers arrested. Ministers imprisoned, some executed, some just disappearing. That man who was killed in the fire? He was a friend of mine. He was a good man. He did nothing to deserve that kind of death.

"Renae, please understand, I'm not saying this to hurt you. I love you. I just want you to know the type of man you are dealing with. I'm not saying this to get you back. If I have lost you, I understand. That's on me. I was a first class jerk. I have to deal with that. I want you to be happy, but I also want you to be safe. And with Jesse, I don't feel you're safe. And I hate it. Remember, I am hurting here too. He was my best friend."

"I have to go." Renae got up and ran out in tears, just as Margaret showed up with Jacob's cheeseburger plate. She raised an eyebrow, but said nothing.

Jacob didn't follow her. He didn't have to. He said what needed saying. The ball was in her court now. At least he was confident she was not part of it. Hopefully, when the time came, he would be the one she would turn to. All he could do now is wait. He lifted his head and made eye contact with a guy in a trucker's hat in the corner booth. Eric nodded back and carried his coffee with him to join Jacob at his booth.

"Thank you for being here," Jacob said. "I appreciate it."

"You okay?"

"I'll be fine. I hated to hurt her like that."

"You did what needed to be done. She was going to be hurt one way or the other. Better coming from a true friend."

"Yeah. Doesn't make it any easier."

"You gonna eat that?" Eric said, pointing at the untouched burger."

"Help yourself. I've lost my appetite."

"Everything will be okay Jacob," Eric said between bites. "I believe that with all my heart."

"Thanks." Jacob laid down a $20, enough for his four cups of coffee and a tip of what he considered as three hours of rent of Margaret's table space.

$$\text{卌 卌 卌 |}$$

Jacob woke up with an odd feeling on Friday morning. The day began normal enough—cup of coffee, an open Bible—but he couldn't seem to focus. Something was off; he just couldn't put a finger on it. He tried to pray, but the words would not form properly, just a jumbled mess of nothingness. He felt flushed. He tried laying down, but couldn't get comfortable. He got up tried to do some routine cleaning but that frustrated him even more. Fuming, he picked up the phone.

"Eric, somethings wrong." Jacob's voice shook. "I don't know how to explain it, but I don't feel… right."

"Are you okay? Do you need a doctor?"

"No, I'm not sick, I just don't feel, I don't know how to describe it… right inside. Like there's a storm about to break but the sky is clear blue, like there is all this pressure, but you can't see it. Something is going to happen. Something big."

"Relax Jacob, take a deep breath," Eric said. "Have you tried praying?"

"Yes, but I can't focus enough for it to make any sense."

"Can I pray with you then?" Eric asked.

"Yes, sure."

Eric paused for a moment. "Lord, I pray for my brother right now. He doesn't understand what he is experiencing right now. I pray that you bring clarity to his mind. Calm his spirit and give him understanding. Show him what is causing this confusion. Shine your light into the darkness and reveal what the enemy is hiding. Give him a solution and the means to carry out what you show him to do. We thank you, Lord. We love you. I ask these things in your name. Amen."

"Amen," Jacob echoed. "Thank you. I do feel better. Still a bit cloudy, but less stressed."

"You're welcome, brother. You going to work today?"

"Yes."

"Remain wary. Don't let down your guard. God puts caution in our hearts; Satan just brings confusion. Remember Paul talking about the armor of God? That's not just a metaphor; it's a spiritual truth. Make sure you are wearing it today. Whether what you're feeling is from God or the adversary, something is coming your way, and you need to be ready for it. I'll keep you in prayer today, even more than I usually do."

"Thanks again. I better get going, or I'll be late."

"God bless, Jacob."

"God Bless."

Jacob did feel more clarity after Eric's prayer. He gulped down the last of his coffee, grabbed his keys from the table, and headed for the door, reciting Paul's litany about putting on the armor of God in his mind. Shield of faith, breastplate of righteousness, helmet of salvation, sword of the spirit—he felt stronger as he mentally donned each piece. It may have been figuratively, but he imagined himself preparing for battle. He felt ready for whatever may be thrown his way.

Jacob must have held his head a little higher than normal, because even Stan wondered about his new attitude. Jacob has always been a hard worker, but now he was attacking each task with an unbridled joy his co-workers hadn't seen before. He is completing tasks ahead of schedule, and even volunteered to help others with their jobs. And his attitude was contagious. Employees actually started smiling at each other.

"Where did this *new* Jacob come from?" Stan cornered him in the break room "I'm not complaining. It's good to see. I just don't get it."

"You know boss; my whole life has been one big mess of negativity. I looked for the bad in everyone, including myself, expecting to find it. And I did. And I was happy to point it out. Not exactly the best recipe for winning friends and influencing people, if you know what I mean. I can no longer live that way. My whole outlook has changed, but I cannot take credit for it. The Lord changed my heart. He has changed my attitude and my work ethic. Now, I'm working as unto Him. I thank you for noticing, but give glory to God, not me."

Stan stood stunned for a moment, then he smiled and said, "Well, I was thinking about giving you a raise, but I guess since God's doing the work, I'll give the raise to God."

"No, I'll take the raise," Jacob laughed. "God don't need it, and I could surely use the extra money."

"Oh, I almost forgot. While you were out on delivery, your wife called." Stan handed him a Post-It with the scrawled message. "I didn't even know you were married."

"Yes, but were separated," Jacob said, grabbing the note.

'Call me ASAP. Don't use a cell phone.'

"I gotta make a phone call, Stan. It's kinda private. Can I use your office?"

"Sure, kid," Stan nodded.

Uneasiness washed over Jacob again, but he couldn't tell if it was a warning from the Holy Spirit, or an attack from the adversary. He went to Stan's office, closed the door behind him, and called Renae. The phone rang several times, then went to voice mail.

'Hello, you've reached Renae. Sorry I missed your call. Wait for the beep! I'll call you back when I can. Bye."

"Renae, it's Jacob. I'll try again later." He hung up and stared at the phone. Fear clinched his throat making it hard to breath. He couldn't wait. He picked up the phone and called again. Three rings and she answered in a whisper.

"Hello, Jake?"

"Yes honey, it's me."

"I can't talk now. Meet me at the Corner Store at 6:00. I'll fill you in then. I gotta go. Bye."

"Renae? Renae?"

She had already hung up.

Jacob looked at the clock on the wall—4:30. He would have to maintain his composure for another hour and a half. He drew in a deep breath, held it, then blew it out slowly. After a quick prayer he left Stan's office and headed back onto the sales floor.

He needed to find something to do to occupy his mind while he waited for his shift to end. There were no more deliveries, but as Stan was fond of saying, *If you got time enough to lean, you got time enough to clean.* He grabbed some paper towels and Windex and wiped down every surface he could find.

While the worked helped the time flow faster, he couldn't get Renae off his mind. The cryptic whispered message worried him. He heard that same tone in Will's voice when he called, just before he died in a fire. He needed to reach her before they did.

He punched out at 5:45 and drove the six blocks to the

Corner Store. He circled the block three times with a meticulous eye. He saw neither a Denali nor any other suspicious vehicle in the vicinity. *When they want to stay hidden, they drive a regular vehicle to blend in,* rang in his ears. He spotted Renae at a gas pump in front of the convenience store, and pulled up to the adjacent pump. He got out and started toward her.

Renae didn't appear to see him, but she loudly whispered, "Don't look at me. Just pretend you're filling up."

Jacob pulled his bank card from his wallet and inserted it into the card reader. "What happened? Are you okay?"

"I'm fine," she whispered back. "No, actually I'm not fine. I'm a wreck."

Jacob looked over to her. "Renae, what happened?"

"Don't look at me. Keep your eyes on filling the tank," she warned again. "Everything you said is true—every bit of it. Jesse is an Official-in-training. He was appointed six months ago. The head guy, Edwards, recruited him. Some Atheist group in Austin is funding Edwards' vendetta. They are providing resources way above what the federal government has allotted. Edwards wants to retire as soon as he finishes completely destroying Eric and his followers. He's tagged Jesse as his heir apparent. But Jesse has to prove himself to the higher ups before he gets the position."

"How do you know all of this?" Jacob said, speaking to his gas tank.

"I came home early from work. Jesse was in the study on the phone. He had Edwards on speaker, so I could hear both clearly. They were talking about the whole plan."

Jacob could hear the tremor in her voice and longed to hold her, comfort her. "What else can you tell me?"

"They knew you and Eric had become close. They have listening devices in the prison cells."

Eric was right; the walls had ears.

"Edwards decided to use me to get to you and Eric. He phoned me to tell me you died. Then he assigned Jesse to *comfort* me through your death…" her voice trailed off again. "His *job* was to seduce me, and turn me against even your memory, so by the time you got out our relationship would be completely destroyed."

"Son of a…" Jacob said.

"Your cellphone is bugged," Renae continued, obviously trying to control the rising anger in her voice. "Jesse does work in an IT capacity, but for Edwards, not some private firm. They can monitor your calls. Both you and Eric. That's why I called you at work."

Jacob nodded. The automatic shut off clicked, and he removed the gas nozzle from his tank.

"One last thing—Jesse wasn't responsible for your friend's death. Edwards had a couple of his deputies do that. Jesse is not a killer. At least, not yet."

"Turner and Anderson," Jacob said under his breath.

"Who?" asked Renae.

"Doesn't matter," Jacob replied. "What else?"

"Edwards thought about letting Eric die in prison. But he realized he could use your friendship with him to take down everyone involved with Eric. Your friend who died in the fire? He was just the first. Jake, I'm scared. I don't know what to do."

"You go on as if nothing happened. You leave here, go home, and say nothing. As Eric always says, the best reaction is no reaction. Whatever happens, please know that I am not the same man you once knew. God had done a miraculous work in my life. I'm sorry for everything I've put you through. When this is over, I pray we can have a second chance."

"I better go," Renae schooled her face to stillness, and replaced the gas nozzle into the pump. "We have already been here for too long. I don't think I can fake filling up any longer."

"Call me at work if you need to," Jacob said without looking at her. "And Renae, I love you."

"I know," she replied. "I love you too."

She got into her car and disappeared over the hill.

Jacob put his gas cap back on and left for his apartment.

In the distance, parked in a darkened lot across the highway, a black Denali idled. It drove off in another direction altogether.

When Jacob arrived at his apartment, a lone figure awaited him, sitting on the steps in front of his door. He couldn't make out his features at first, but he didn't need to. The black Denali in the parking lot gave him away. It was Jesse.

"Your home late."

"I needed gas. Was running on fumes. Everything okay?"

"Of course. Why wouldn't everything be okay?" Jesse's smile indicated everything wasn't okay.

"No reason. Just wasn't expecting you." Jacob unlocked his door and invited Jesse in. "I don't have much in the fridge, but I could offer you a bottled water."

"Oh, I won't be long," Jesse said. He looked around the apartment, almost identical to the way Edwards had on his visit. "I just wanted to check on you. See if you needed anything. I've been in and out of town so much since we last talked. Just wanted to catch up."

"I'm good. Working over at Stan's. Keeps me busy, and gainfully employed." Jacob sat on the couch.

"Yes, I heard he needed a good part-time worker."

"Yeah, it seems a good match. He needed help, and I needed a job," His sarcasm seeping through. "And I am full time."

"Is that right? Then it definitely worked out then." Jesse met Jacob's eyes. "I also heard you have met with Renae a couple of times."

"Wasn't trying to keep it a secret. She is still my wife after all." Jacob met Jesse stare for stare, with more heat than he intended. *So much for the best reaction being no reaction.*

"Calm down, man. I didn't come here to start a fight." As if to punctuate his statement, Jesse took a step back and folded his arms, his biceps bulging under his white uniform shirt. "But you need to understand that she is with me now. Please, let her move on. You lost her a long time ago, way before you were put in prison. It was your words, your actions that pushed her into my arms."

The heat in Jacob's eyes reverted to a holy fire. He wasn't sure where the words came from, but he was pretty sure they weren't from him. "I realize that Jesse. And just as I have apologized to you, I gave her the same speech. I have changed. God has changed me. If neither of you can believe it, I must accept that. But I truly am sorry for the pain I have caused. That was the subject of our meetings, not an attempt to win her back. Yes, I still love her; I always will. But whether she decides to come back to me or stay with you—that's up to her. It's not up to me. And it's most certainly not up to you."

Jesse smirked, "Just as long as you keep to that. She's in enough pain right now as it is. No need for you to make things worse."

"I understand." Jacob walked to the door and opened it. "Thanks for stopping by. I appreciate your concern. I had forgotten what a good friend you've always been to me."

Jesse shrugged as he walked out. "Just being there for you, Jacob."

Jacob closed the door and locked it. He turned and examined his apartment, looking for anything out of place. *If they can bug the phones, Lord knows what they can do to my apartment.* He started to call Eric. *That's stupid. Bugged, remember?* He examined his cellphone but didn't see anything out of the ordinary. Perhaps they were intercepting the signal somehow? Jesse was always good with electronics, and with government resources at his fingertips, he could…

"Damn!" he swore. "Eric. The meeting." Jacob peeked through the curtains. Jesse's Denali was still in the parking lot. He was trapped. No way out; no way to call Eric without being overheard. He snapped his fingers.

He grabbed his cell and dialed. Before Eric could even say 'hello,' Jacob blurted, "Hey, Eric. It's Jacob. Look, I'm not going to make it for dinner tonight. Lunch didn't agree with me and I'm afraid I'm gonna throw up. I'm sorry. I will call you tomorrow." He made groaning sounds as he disconnected the call, hoping Eric would take the hint.

He looked through the curtains again. The Denali was still there. *Better him stalking me than harassing Renae. Proceed as if nothing was wrong. Normal routine.* He popped a Hungry Man into the microwave and turned on the TV. The eight o'clock news was just beginning.

"We would like to update you on a story we brought to you last week on fire at an auto body shop in New Braunfels. William Anderson lost his life in the fire. Arson investigators have

completed their investigation and determined that a leaking compressed gas tank ignited while Anderson was working on a car in his shop. With no evidence of foul play, authorities are ruling this a tragic accident. In other news..."

Well played, Edwards. Jacob lost his appetite. When the microwave beeped for him, he ignored it. He turned the TV off and headed to his bedroom. He laid down in the growing darkness and stared up at the ceiling. The ceiling fan played with the last rays of light filtering in through the blinds creating a steady, mesmerizing strobe effect that lulled him toward slumber.

He missed his friend.

He missed his wife.

He missed his son.

It's in God's hands now, he reminded himself as he drifted into sleep.

卌 卌 卌 ||

"Jacob," Stan called from the back office. "Come here a moment."

"Yeah boss?"

"There's a box in the back that needs to go to Mills Motors. Can you run it over before the end of your shift?

"I'm already there," Jacob replied, then added, "actually, I have that invoicing you wanted me to do from the new shipment. Would it be alright if I ran it by there on my way home?"

"That'll work."

Invoicing. I hate invoicing. Match the orders with what's actually in the box. Check counts, verify model numbers, make allowance for special orders, yeesh, it's enough to drive a crazy man sane! Jacob fancied himself as more of a hands-on type of guy. *Gimme something to do, and I'll do it, but dealing with numbers all day, not my cup of tea.* Skimming down the manifest, he came across the order for Mills Motors. Six Mason Car Charger Adapters. *Interesting.* Jacob finalized all invoices. Nothing missing or short. All was in line with what was ordered. He grabbed the box with *MM* printed on the top and headed out.

Since it was after hours, it was quiet at Mills Motors, but Jacob was surprised to see a couple of familiar cars parked along the side of the building, including Frank's Chevy and

Eric's Ford. He looked around for any sign of unwanted company as he walked up to the entrance. The bell sounded as he entered, and Jessica walked out of the back office to greet him. "Howdy, Jacob. We were wondering when you'd get here."

"I waited till the end of my shift. Didn't want to deliver and run."

"Wonderful. Then you can join us in the back. Service is about to start."

"Really? Just in time then."

Jacob followed Jessica to the back. Frank and Roger were up against a rack of tires that lined the wall. Eric sat at a makeshift podium normally used for service ticket writing, scribbling in a book. He glanced up and said, "Jacob! So glad you could make it." He came over and gave him a handshake and a hug.

"How have you been, Eric?"

"Good, good. God is good," he said with a smile. "I understood your message yesterday. We had to cancel last night's meeting anyhow. Edwards' Denali was parked outside my place. A gray one was sitting in Roger's parking lot, and Frank was out of town. He just got back this afternoon. I called everyone here for a quick, emergency meeting. It appears they are somehow gaining inside information on our meetings."

"I believe I know how." Jacob explained his conversation with Renae.

"Wow," Frank said. "Who'd a thought we were all that important? I mean, don't these guys have bigger fish to fry? Why dedicate all these resource to us?"

"Guys, I am afraid for Renae," Jacob confessed. "I want your permission to bring her into our group. I feel we could better protect her if she were part of what we are doing."

"Is she clean?" Frank asked.

"Yes, she is innocent. I know it in my heart. Edwards is using Jesse's relationship with her to get to Eric, but she knew nothing about it until I brought it up."

"What I've seen is good enough for me," said Eric. "Feel free to bring her by anytime. But be careful."

"Always," Jacob said. "Speaking of caution, I assume that's what these are for?" Jacob handed Roger the box.

"Ah! I was hoping they came in," Roger said snapping his utility knife open.

"Car charger adapters?" Jacob laughed.

"Well, listing them as *cell phone bug detectors* on the invoice didn't seem prudent to me," Roger said. He opened the box and pulled out six identical smaller boxes. "One for each of us."

"But there are only five of us," Jacob said, realizing Will would not need one now.

"One if for Renae," Eric said.

Jacob raised an eyebrows. "How did you know—"

"The other day at Maggie's. I'm not blind, Jacob. It was obvious she was authentically fearful. You confirmed her innocence. It was only a matter of time before she discovered the truth. To be honest, I'm glad she found out sooner than later. Now we can work with her, instead of trying to work around her."

"You don't have to worry about her," Jacob vouched for his wife. "You're right; she is just as afraid as we are."

"Let's begin," Eric said, adjusting his glasses and flipping through the pages of his notebook. "We all know that Will is now in a better place. He is running around Heaven right now giving bear hugs to Peter and Paul and skipping rocks along the crystal sea with David and Elijah. While we mourn his passing, we also rejoice in his homegoing. Praise be to God!"

"Amen, Pastor!" Jessica said, and everyone echoed agreement.

"What I'd like to talk about tonight is the battle ahead of us. I still owe each of you a debt of gratitude for sticking by me. I know you are standing up for the Lord, but doing it with this church, that God has allowed me to pastor, means a lot to me. I know it feels like we are alone in this battle. But remember, we are not fighting against a man or any group of men. Our enemy is Satan and his angels who are working *through* those individuals.

"*For we are not fighting against flesh-and-blood enemies, but against evil rulers and authorities of the unseen world, against mighty powers in this dark world, and against evil spirits in the heavenly places.*

"If our battle is not with them, but with powers and principalities in spiritual realms, then we cannot presume to do battle in the strength of human effort. Only God can fight these battles. Only He can bring victory. He has already brought the victory. We only need to stand. Never giving up or giving in. Ask God for the strength. Never doubt, for as James 1:6 says:

"*But when you ask, you must believe and not doubt, because the one who doubts is like a wave of the sea, blown and tossed by the wind.*

"We cannot take this on half-hearted. We cannot fear, because God is in control and He ensures our victory. Our eyes and hearts need to turn to him for strength, and to fill us with his Spirit so we will endure until the final enemy falls in defeat."

Jacob was on the edge of his seat. Ready. Empowered. His spirit on fire and ready for whatever came next.

"So, what's next you may ask?" Eric reads Jacob's mind. "We pray. We can see the enemy encamping around us and staging their pieces for a final battle. It's coming soon, my friends. We must stand strong in the faith. Let our departed brother be a prime example. If he hadn't given his life defending us, this place here would be in a pile of rubble as well.

"We fight this next battle on our knees. We pray. We pray as we have never prayed before. We pray for our enemies, that their eyes will be opened to the evil around them, that they come to their senses, that they find a relationship with the almighty God. If Jesus could pray for those who were crucifying him, then we can pray for those who are seeking our lives as well."

"Amen!" Roger shouted.

"I'm excited," Eric said. "How 'bout y'all?"

"Let's do this!" Jessica said.

"First, a little practical instruction. Let me show you how these detectors work," Roger said. "It's fairly simple. It will let you know anytime your cell phone is transmitting information. Just turn it on and place it near your cell phone. Green is good, red is bad. Officials can covertly turn on your phone's microphone and listen, but with this, you can easily see if they are actively listening. Red means your phone is active."

"Make sure you get it going before you leave here," Eric explained. "If you can't figure it out, ask Roger for help. We can't risk all of us getting caught together."

Roger added, "We don't need to worry when you're here. This building has RF shielding. It won't allow signals to penetrate it. You can thank the old Soviet Union for that small favor. Wi-Fi still allows outgoing calls to work; there is a shield on that too, so they can't track us through the signal. You're safe here."

"Thank you, Pastor," Frank said.

"Yes. Thank you both," Jacob echoed.

"Here ya go, Jacob. Two units. One for you and one for Renae."

"Where did you get these? I wasn't aware that anything like this existed."

Roger smiled. "That's my secret. I can't reveal my sources."

"Roger, Roger." Jacob joked.

"One last thing everyone," Eric added. "I've been praying about direction. I don't want to say anything about it yet, because I don't have confirmation from God about it. But I would surely appreciate your prayers."

"No problem," Jacob said.

"You got it," Jessica echoed.

"Amen Pastor," both Frank and Roger said.

"Until next time, keep a sharp eye out. Remember, the battle belongs to the Lord, but we must still be wary. Good night gentleman… and lady," Eric said, grinning. He folded up his notebook and made his exit.

Frank and Jessica followed close behind leaving Roger and Jacob in the shop. Roger stuck his hands in his front pockets as and fidgeted, as if wrestling with whether or not to say something. Jacob noticed and said, "Out with it. You look like you're about to explode."

Roger nodded. "All right. You asked for it. I just wanted to let you know that, well, marriage is tough under the best conditions. These days, it's a wonder any marriage survives.

But, I can tell you from experience, anything in a marriage can be overcome."

Jacob blew out a surprised breath. He wasn't expecting that. "I don't know," he fumbled for words. "I've caused a lot of damage to mine. I have no right to even ask, much less expect, Renae to forgive me."

"None of us deserve forgiveness, Jacob. That's the beauty of grace. Trust me, all hell could break out, but if God is at the center of a marriage, that marriage can be saved. It's the people in the marriage who give up, not God. There is hope for you and Renae. Don't give up. Pray for her. When you see her again, pray *with* her. There is nothing like a man who not afraid to show humility before his wife. God honors that. She will respect that."

"Thank you, Roger," Jacob said. "That means a lot. I better get going. Just in case she tries to call tonight. Oh, I almost forgot." Jacob pulled a folded piece of paper from his shirt pocket and handed it to Roger. He clicked his pen and said, "Sign here please." It was the invoice for the box he delivered.

卌 卌 卌 III

"I don't know, Jacob," Renae said, wiping tears from her eyes. "I'm afraid. Jesse scares me. But I've already accepted him into my home, and he takes care of Michael. How can I leave him alone with our son now knowing what I know?"

"Does he suspect that you know anything?"

"I don't think so." Renae picked up a napkin from the break room table and dabbed her eyes.

"Take some PTO and go visit with your parents for a while," Jacob suggested. "Tell him one of them is ill, or that you just really miss them."

"What if he suspects something? He knows that we've talked."

"I'll make sure his focus is on me. Just let me know when you are ready, and I'll take care of it."

"How do I get word to you?"

"Leave a message for me at my work, like last time. Give your name and tell them to hold a part you ordered because you're going out of town and the dates you'll be gone."

Renae nodded, struggling to hold back a fresh flow of tears.

Jacob took her hand. "Look at me."

Renae turned to him, and their eyes met. The irritation evident there since his return from prison was gone. It was replaced by a combination of emotions: fear, anxiety, a tentative hope and what appeared to be the stirrings of the love she once had for him, beginning to rise again. It was guarded, but it was there. She gently squeezed his hand.

"Everything is going to be okay," Jacob said. He raised her hand to his lips. "I will keep you safe. I promise. There is one other thing I'd like to ask you to do."

"What is it?"

"I would like for you to go with me to a meeting Eric is having. I guess you could call it a church service. There's just a few of us, people you may already know in town—Roger and Jessica Mills, Frank Dunham, Eric, and myself."

"I know Roger and Jessica, and Mr. Dunham. Both have business accounts with us."

"Great, then you should feel comfortable."

"Where is it?"

"That I can't tell you," Jacob said. "Plausible deniability. Remember, Eric and I are being watched. If Jesse does happen to ask, you can honestly say you don't know."

"I understand. When is the meeting?"

"This evening after work. We try to meet once a week. The days vary depending on schedules. Usually around 6:00. It doesn't last long, 7:00 or 7:30 at the latest. You can come straight from work. I will let you know where right before you leave."

"I better get back to work," Renae said, looking up at the clock. "Thank you for coming. I appreciate it."

"Of course. And I need to get back to the shop." Jacob leaned in to kiss her on the cheek, but Renae turned her head, and allowed their lips to meet.

"You have no idea how long I've waited for this moment," Jacob murmured.

Renae smiled. "I've missed it too."

"I'll talk with you later, my love." Jacob was pretty sure his feet never touched the floor as he walked out of the bank. He floated all the way back to his job. If everything went south at this moment, Jacob knew he would die a happy man. For the first time in a long time, he was joyful. He didn't feel the weight of the world pressing down on his shoulders. The future looked bright, and he couldn't wait to see what God would do next.

As excited as Jacob was, business at work had devolved into a slow drudgery. There were no deliveries to make, nothing left to clean that he hadn't clean twice already. Even invoicing was caught up. *Ah, sweet Lord, could this day drag any slower?*

The only thing that helped was the anticipation of seeing Renae again. He couldn't wait to introduce her to Eric. He wanted her to see how much he has changed. He even dared to hope that they might find a way to regain their life together. *Forget about Jesse; I'm getting my wife and son back. Even if I have to fight for her, there's no price I won't pay.*

As closing time approached, Jacob prepared a distraction for Jesse. He turned on the device Roger gave him and placed near his phone. A red light lit up; his cell was being monitored, *Perfect.* He dialed Eric, knowing his phone would most likely be off. He left a message, "Hey Eric, it's Jacob. Look, this whole Will thing is still getting to me. I'm going up to his shop and dig around a bit to see if I can find anything. I'm already on my way, so I won't be able to meet you for dinner. Don't worry; I'm not driving my truck. I'll call you tomorrow with an update on what I find."

There. That should keep him busy.

Jacob went into the office and picked up the landline. He called Renae at the bank. "First Commerce Bank, this is

Renae. How can I provide excellent service for you today?"

"Renae, it's Jacob," he whispered.

"Hey Jacob, do you have a place for me yet?"

"Yes, meet over at Mills Motors. There is a path that runs along the right side of the building that will take you to the back. Park back there, as far back as possible to keep your car out of sight of the street. And double check that you are not being followed. You don't have to worry about Jesse; he's going to be out of town."

"Yes, I know. He just texted me that he had to go on an emergency run to help a client."

"Perfect."

"What time again?"

"Six-thirty."

"I'll be there. I gotta go. I need to finish closing out the tellers."

"See you in a bit. I love you."

"Love you too, Jake."

She called me Jake. Jacob smiles.

He hung up the phone and finished his own closing paperwork. There were several deliveries on the schedule for the next day. As he was planning out his route, he came across two invoices for familiar customers. The first was for Mills Motors. That box was ready for delivery, so he grabbed it. *No sense making an extra stop tomorrow when I can deliver it tonight.*

The second was more problematic. It was addressed to the local federal law enforcement substation; Recipient: Official Nathan Edwards. The item's description was 'Personal and Confidential.' Special instructions read: 'Client requests Jacob Andrews as delivery driver.'

Well, that's one way to get someone's attention.

Jacob pondered the package. It didn't look threatening. It was about the size of a tissue box. Other than the FRAGILE label, it was normal in every sense of the word. He couldn't begin to guess what it could contain. The sender was Tungsten Leather. They made fancy bling for cars: steering wheel covers, seat covers, floor mats, and such. He set the package aside and grabbed the much larger box for Mills. It was labeled *Apox*. They sold car stereos—ones with detachable faces, very old school. He signed on the paperwork that the package had been delivered and headed out the door. Although he felt safe, it didn't stop him from giving a thorough once around before he left the lot. If he was stopped, he had a package, that would be his story.

Jacob pulled up to Mills Motors and parked. Renae was already there, waiting. Her hair was up in a bun and her sunglasses propped on top of her head. Jacob thought she looked amazing.

"Is this okay?" she asked, obviously nervous.

"You're fine," Jacob said with a smile. "Let's go on in."

Jacob led the way to the rear of the shop, and opened the door. They could hear Frank playing "Old Rugged Cross" on his guitar. Hearing it made Renae smile.

"Not something you'd expect to hear out of an auto shop, right?" Jacob joked.

"I like it," she said. "It reminds me of when I was a little girl. Dad would play his records after supper."

"That you, Jacob?" shouted Roger from around a rack of tires.

"Yes, and I've brought a friend."

"It's me, Mr. Mills. Renae from the bank."

"Renae?" Jessica's voice could be heard from the office, but unseen.

"Heya, Jessica." Renae looked over to the office, then back to Jacob.

"Go say hello."

Renae smiled and headed for the office, while Jacob walked across to the shop floor. "Sounds good, Frank."

"She needs a tune-up," he said, adjusting one of the tuning pegs. He plucked a couple of times and gave it a good strum. He smiled and the brim of his hat raised with his eyebrows. "Much better." Frank looked over toward the office, "Glad to see you were able to bring the Mrs. Makes my heart glad that you two are patching things up."

"Our marriage is a far cry from being patched up, Frank," Jacob said. "But we're trying. I think we're making progress."

"Making up is the fun part," Frank said with a sly wink, "I'm sure Roger has told you, he and Jessica had some issues several years back. Back before Eleanore went to be with the Lord— Eleanore was my wife, if you didn't know—she was a brilliant counselor. She helped them both; now they are stronger than ever. You need some good folk to talk to, they would be the ones."

The shop door opened again, and Roger called out "Eric, is that you?"

"Yes, brother, it is I," he called back.

"Gimme a minute. These tires aren't going to inventory themselves."

Eric walked up to Frank and Jacob and greeted them both with firm handshakes.

"You're in a good mood," Jacob says.

"I'm still above ground, we get to fellowship, and God is still on the throne. What's not to be in a good mood about? And even if the first two weren't true, He is still on the throne."

"Not to put a damper on things, but I have to make a special delivery tomorrow. To Official Edwards," Jacob said. "There's an order for him at the store, and they specifically requested that I be the one to deliver it."

Eric nodded. "You alone?" he asked.

"No," Jacob answered with a smile. "Renae is in the office with Jessica."

"Ahh," Eric elbowed Jacob and pointed toward the office. "Chick-chat."

The men chuckled. "Who knows how long they will be," Roger said as he joined the men. He had a clipboard in one hand and a rag in the other, black streaks ran down his face. "Well, that's that. Tires are done." Spying the box under Jacob's arm. "That for me?"

"As a matter of fact, it is." Jacob handed the box to him.

"Awesome. I wasn't expecting them till tomorrow."

"Yeah, it's on tomorrow's roster for delivery, but I saw it and figured since I was headed this way anyway..."

"Thank you. Timing couldn't be better," Roger said. He set the box down on the makeshift podium, pulled out his utility knife, and sliced through the sealing tape. Inside the box were a dozen cell phones. "Burners," he explained. "Each of us gets one. Let's see 'em track us now."

"I didn't realize Apox made cell phones," Jacob said.

Roger gave a mischievous grin. "They don't."

"I'm not even going to ask," Jacob said.

"Best you don't. Ask me no questions, I'll tell you no lies."

Renae followed Jessica out of the office and into the shop where the men were congregating.

Eric said, "You must be Renae."

Renae blushed and nodded.

"I've heard much about you. You are every bit as beautiful as Jacob has told me. It is a pleasure to meet you finally." He extended his hand to her and she shook it. "Well, the gang is all here. Shall we begin?"

Frank played a couple of worship songs and an old hymn, then Eric prayed before delivering a sermon about walking in the steps of Christ. As much as Jacob appreciated Eric's sermons, he spent most of the time furtively watching Renae. He could tell she was enjoying herself. She had that bright-eyed look he remembered when she used to drive past him when he was nothing but a field hand.

As the service started drawing to a close, Eric decided to make one more announcement. "I am convinced the Lord is calling me to hold an open service. I love our little group here, but if we remain just us, how are we ever going to impact our community, our culture, our world? I know trouble awaits, but that should not stop us. I believe the time has come for us to take a stand, to say to our community that we are followers of Christ. We were called to shine a light; we can't do that by hiding in the dark."

The room was silent. Jacob wondered if everyone else was as excited and nervousness as he was.

"When?" Roger asked.

"Next Sunday," Eric answered. "I have been given the opportunity to examine a building at the abandoned High School in Polk. We'll start by inviting people we know to this service, and encourage them to invite others. We will send a message that the Lord's message will not be silenced."

Eric stopped speaking, and the room remained quiet for a long moment.

Jacob stood, "Pastor, I am with you all the way."

"If Jake is in, I'm in," Renae stood next to him taking his hand.

"Don't think I'm not in Pastor, not for one second," Frank echoed his support.

"Roger?" Eric looked his way.

Roger looked at Jessica. She smiled; he smiled. "There is no way we would miss this."

"Then it is unanimous." A determined smile crossed Eric's face. "This is how it begins, one small act of defiance at a time that declares to the powers, authorities, and principalities in high places, *We will not go quietly into the night.*"

$$\cancel{||||}\ \cancel{||||}\ \cancel{||||}\ ||||$$

Jacob looked over his itinerary for the day. He tried to put off the delivery to the Official Edwards as long as he could, but there was no way to avoid it. It would be his second delivery after lunch. At least the order didn't require a signature. *I could just leave the package at the front desk, but where would that get me? Like Eric said, it's time to take a stand, to let them know I'm not afraid anymore.*

He pulled up to the office a little after 12:30. He let the truck idling for a minute. He couldn't tell if the rattling he heard was the engine or his heart. Paralyzing fear gripped him. A swirl of thoughts assaulted him. *What do you think you're doing? You can't stand up to Edwards. He tazed you. He had you beaten and thrown into jail. What makes you think you're up to this challenge. You're a weak coward. You should just drive away. Keep driving. Don't come back.* Then a still small voice whispered in his ear. *Fear not.*

The voices in his head increased in volume, became insistent, pleading, demanding, whining.

Fear not!

Jacob knew the owner of that voice. He reached for the door handle and stepped out of the truck. The cacophony of voices swirled away as quickly as they came. He stepped out onto the street and made his way to the building. Just as he reached for the door a familiar voice called out from behind him.

"That must be for me."

Jacob turned. "Yes, sir." He held the package out.

Edwards didn't take it. Instead he opened the door and stepped through, holding it open for Jacob. "Follow me, Mr. Andrews," he said, crooking his finger to direct Jacob to the back office.

"I have other deliveries to make, Official Edwards. I don't have much time."

"I won't keep you long, Mr. Andrews. "You'll be on your way soon enough."

Once in the office, Edwards pointed to a leather chair in front of a large oak desk. Jacob sat, the box he was still carrying was on his lap. Jacob glanced around the office while he waited for Edwards to get to the point of their meeting, or whatever this was. Framed diplomas and certificates of appreciation from law enforcement to community service. One shadow box held a badge with an engraved bronze plate proclaiming: "Atlanta Major Crimes Division."

"That badge is what got me here." Edwards said, noticing Jacob's interest in it. "Your friend Eric knows all about it. By now I suspect you do too. At least, you know his side of the story." He opened a box on top of his desk and pulled out a cigar. He inhaled the aroma of the fine Cuban tobacco and smiled. "Ah, wonderful. It's the little things that make life worth living. Would you care for one?"

"No, thank you," Jacob said.

"Of course not. You've found that old time religion, haven't you Mr. Andrews. *You don't smoke and you don't chew and don't go with girls who do*, right?" He clipped the end of the cigar and put it in his mouth. He struck a wooden match and started to raise it, then stopped as if remembering something important. He shook the flame from the matchstick and dropped it into the ashtray on his desk. "Where were we? Ah yes, Mr. Lassiter's version of the events in Atlanta. Would you like to hear my version?"

"I've heard enough," Jacob chimed.

"Oh, but you haven't heard enough. Don't you know, Mr. Andrews, *You will know the truth, and the truth shall set you free?* Well, it's time you heard the truth. Did you know that Mr. Lassiter's blatant disregard for the rights of others almost cost me my badge?" Edwards explained, pointing his cigar toward the shadowbox. "No one wanted to touch that case. I was the only one with big enough cojones to even pick up the file." Edwards leaned forward, his voice taking on the intensity of a Ringling Brothers carnival barker. "Lassiter wasn't concerned for the emotional strain he was putting people under. No sir, he didn't care for their right to live as they saw fit. He only wanted to change them, for his own glory, position, and power.

"Mr. Andrews, people have the right to live however they want to live, without fear of being belittled, criticized, made to feel less than human. And for some Christian," he sneered, "to have the gall to demand that people live by a certain set rules is heinous. I've experienced that kind of religious repression in my own life, and I was fed up. So, when the Atlanta case, I jumped at the chance to right an egregious wrong.

"No one else took it seriously. Most of the attorneys in my office felt there wasn't even a case. My precinct chief all but ordered me to leave it alone. But you know what I did? I took the case."

Jacob held the package so tightly that his fingers began to cramp. Inside he could feel his soul clinching. The longer

Edwards talked, the more Jacob felt his old nature rising up. Everything in him wanted to smart off, to make a snarky retort, to call the man a bold-faced liar. He had not felt the urge to express his feelings since his release from prison. Then again, he hadn't been tested by someone he detested as much as he despised Official Edwards. Instead of unleashing his vitriol, Jacob closed his eyes and prayed for strength and wisdom. All he really wanted at this moment was to give Edwards his package and leave.

"No one really won or lost that case," Edwards droned on. "Oh, the judge gave Lassiter a slap on the wrist. A fine. A measly fine! No jail time. No restitution for the emotional damage he'd caused to my client. Not to mention all the time, energy, and work I put into that case. Idiot judge. He said that there was nothing he could to do. There was no precedent, he ruled. *I sympathize with the plaintiff, but my hands are tied,*" Edwards mocked.

Jacob could contain himself no long. "But you're the one who went on to fight for that precedent. You're the one responsible for changing the law and ruining the lives of people of faith."

"I ruined *their* lives?!" A scarlet flush crept up Edwards' face and he shook his fist in the air. Jacob thought he might be having a heart attack. "What about the lives these *preachers* have destroyed? These fish-belly white, pedagogues with their rules and regulations. *Touch not, taste not, handle not.* These prissy, holier-than-thou Puritans, who only want to control people so they can get their money. *Oh, give till it hurts, then keep on giving till it starts to feel good!* These self-righteous, sanctimonious Bible thumpers. *Turn or burn!* they shout. What kind of god sends people to everlasting hell? Tell me that? These perpetrators of piety spew fear and hatred. They are an abomination! They are a crime against nature, against humanity! They must be crushed!" he said as he crushed his cigar in his fist.

His diatribe exhausted, Edwards sat back in his chair, breathing in short, ragged gasps.

"I'm sorry, sir," Jacob swallowed hard. "I don't see it that way."

"Of course you don't," Edwards nodded. He motioned for Jacob to hand him the package. Jacob was glad to have it out of his hands. He flexed his fingers to work the blood back into them. "You've been blinded by Mr. Lassiter's calm demeanor, his soothing acceptance—just as you are. But he hides a dark secret. I hope our little discussion here helps clear things up for you."

Edwards stood and walked around Jacob, looking him over from front to back, top to bottom. He let out a disappointed grunt as he walked back to his desk and sat. "What happened to you, citizen? You used to be bold. You used to be aggressive. You used to be a man. You took what I dished out and gave it back, tit-for-tat. Yes, you were a pain in the butt, and you pissed me off, but I liked that about you. What happened to that guy?"

Edwards pick up the letter opener on his desk and sliced through the tape on the edges of the box. He shoved the tissue packing aside. The musky aroma of leather wafted through the room. He pulled out an elegantly tooled, handmade holster. He smiled. "Ah, yes. She's a beauty." He opened the top drawer of his desk and lifted out a gleaming, silver .45 caliber revolver. Pulling a handkerchief from his jacket pocket, he lovingly polished the barrel, the cylinder, the handle. "You see Mr. Andrews, most of the time I really enjoy my job. It's not all that difficult. There are excellent benefits. And I get to do something I truly love."

Edwards stopped polishing his revolver and pointed the barrel straight at Jacob. "But little pricks like you—you get my goat. One minute you're this cocky, bantam rooster with chip on his shoulder that I can't stand, but can't help but admire. Next minute you're this soft-spoken, level-headed, pantywaist pacifist who shrinks from a fight rather than standing his ground. Bottom line, Mr. Andrews—I can't figure you out. I don't like things I can't figure out. It's very upsetting."

"I'm sorry to disappoint you," Jacob said. He felt a heat surging through his spirit. "I understand how you feel. I truly do! I was once like you, convinced that there was nothing and nobody who cared about me, and no deity watching from on high to either deliver me from my trials and tribulations or flinging lightning bolts at me if I did something wrong.

"Honestly, I'm not that hard to figure out. I simply had a genuine encounter with God; a loving God who gave me a second chance at life. In the bravado of my old life, I used to hurt people, even people I cared about. I don't want to be that guy anymore. I don't want to tear people down. I want to lift them up, to challenge them to be better than they are. That's not hate, Official Edwards. Wanting what is best for another person is the highest form of love you can display."

"You are insane, citizen," Edwards replied. He slipped the revolver into his new holster and affixed it to his belt. Then he looked directly at Jacob and smiled. "Oh, and citizen? You should remember who it is you are speaking to."

"With all due respect, Official Edwards, I know exactly who I am speaking to," Jacob said. "You mentioned admiring that guy who stood up to you, and now you think I'm afraid because I don't shout or call you names. The truth is, I don't need to raise my voice or my hand. Your threats simply don't scare me anymore." He paused, allowing an unfamiliar, but completely welcome sense of well-being flow through his body.

"It's funny," he continued. "Driving over here, all I could think about was how afraid I was. You can be very intimidating, Official Edwards. But now, after our little chat, I finally understand what Eric meant when he encouraged me to not fear the one who can kill the body, but has no power over the soul. So kill me if you're going to kill me. Bottom line, Mr. Edwards—I still win. I know the condition of my soul. You pull that trigger, I know without a doubt where I'll go. Can you say the same."

Fury flashed in Edwards' eyes, but an incredulous smile that never reached those eyes creased his face. "Pull the trigger? Citizen, I'm not going to shoot you. Oh, my no! I have much bigger plans for you—and for that pretty little wife of yours."

"What is that supposed to mean," Jacob's jaw dropped.

"Don't act so innocent, Mr. Andrews. I know you two are sweetening things up. Poor Jesse though. So sad for him to learn the woman he is living with is putting out with another man. Even if that other man is her husband."

"You leave her alone. Whatever this is, it's between you and me. She has nothing to do with it."

"Of course she does." Edwards leaned back, steepling his fingers in front of his face. "After all, she holds the key to you heart."

Jacob rose to his full height. Any warm, fuzzy feelings he might have had were shoved down, replaced by pure, unadulterated, holy fury. He leaned over Edwards' desk and pointed his finger between Edwards' eyes. "Touch her, and I will end you." Jacob took a step back without breaking their eye-lock. "I have wasted enough time here. I have deliveries to make. Good day—Sir."

卌 卌 卌 卌

Jacob sat straight up in bed, startled awake. *Deep breaths, Andrews. It was just a dream. Weird, though.* With this heart rate back to normal, Jacob laid down and tried to go back to sleep, but the abrupt ending to his dream kept playing like a nickelodeon in his head. He stared at the ceiling for a while, willing his eyes to close, but to no avail. Finally, he kicked off the covers and walked to the kitchen for a glass of water.

The flickering digital readout on the stove indicated it was 2:23 a.m. He returned the glass to the cabinet, *it was just water, no need to wash it*, he reasoned, and started back for the bedroom, when his cellphone when off. Middle of the night calls were never good news. He ran down the hall and snatched the phone from its charger.

"Hello?"

"Jacob, I am sorry about the hour, but I just had the craziest dream, and I couldn't wait until morning to talk with you about it." Eric sounded the way Jacob felt—agitated, confused, perhaps a bit excited, but definitely unable to sleep.

"No worries. It's fine. I was already up," Jacob said. "In fact, I just had a crazy dream, too. And it was about you."

"Really? Mine was about you. Did it involve walking down a path in the rain?"

"How did you—"

"Do you work tomorrow?"

"No, I'm off."

"Meet me at Maggie's in a half-hour. We need to talk about this in person."

"Yeah, sure. Just let me get dressed."

"Yes. See you in a bit."

Jacob threw on a pair of sweats and a hoodie and headed toward Maggie's. *What in the world is so important about a weird dream about walking in the rain, that it can't wait until morning,* he grumbled to himself. Not that he would be able to sleep any more tonight anyway.

By the time Jacob walked into the restaurant, Eric was already there, sitting in a back corner booth, far from where they usually sat. He was staring at his coffee cup. Inside the diner was warm, with the comforting smell of chicken fried steak permeating the air. Margaret met him as he walked in.

"What can I do for ya sweetie?" She carried a smile and a carafe of hot coffee.

"Don't you ever go home, Margaret?" Jacob asked.

"When you own the joint, days off are few and far between," she laughed. "I wouldn't have it any other way. Can I sit you somewhere?"

"No, I'm meeting Pastor Eric. I see him back there. I could sure go for a cup of coffee."

"Slice of pie as well? Fresh blackberry cobbler today."

"Sounds wonderful."

"Comin' right up." She grabbed an empty cup and headed to the booth just ahead of Jacob.

"Top ya off, Pastor?" she asked while she filled Jacob's cup.

"Yes ma'am. Keep it coming."

"I'll be right back with y'all's cobbler."

Once Margaret was out of earshot, Jacob asked, "How are you doing, Pastor?"

"That's a little formal at this stage of the game, don't you think? Call me Eric."

"Okay. So, how are you doing—Eric?" Jacob smiled.

"I'm sorry to pull you out of bed at this time of night. It's not my normal MO. But when I learned we had the same dream; sleep seemed insignificant."

"What's so important about a dream, even if we did happen to have similar dreams?" Jacob asked.

"Sometimes a dream is just a dream. But sometimes, it's more," Eric explained. The Bible is filled with stories about God speaking to men through their dreams. Jacob, Joseph, Pharaoh, Solomon, Nebuchadnezzar, Daniel, even Pontius Pilate's wife had dreams that were from God. The key was properly interpreting those dreams. One of the prophecies in the Book of Acts was that *your young men will see visions, and your old men will dream dreams.*"

"So now you're saying I'm an old man?" Jacob quipped.

Eric smiled. "The point is that if God has given us the same dream; I believe He may be trying to tell us something. I wanted to compare our dreams while they were still fresh in our memories; how they are alike, what's different. The fact that you were in my dream and I was in yours tells me that's significant. Tell me about your dream. Every detail, not matter how small, could be important."

"Okay, I'm game." Jacob thought for a moment, took a long sip of his coffee, and began. "It was late, in the wee hours of the morning. It was raining, hard—no it was pouring, like a cloudburst. The rain made it difficult to see. You were walking through a field that came up to a path. The only thing you had to light your way was a lantern—one of those old-style Coleman lanterns with a wire handle on the top my dad used to take when we went camping. The wind was whipping, rocking it back and forth.

"You were wearing a black rain slicker," Jacob continued, his eyes closed, seeing every detail as if dreaming it again. "And you wore a large, flat-brimmed hat that the wind tried to blow off, but couldn't. As the grass cleared beneath your feet, you were on a caliche path. Then, you came up to a gate, like one of those gates I told you about several weeks ago, a five-barred gate. You came up to the gate and pushed on it, but it didn't open. You lifted on the latch and pushed again. It didn't budge. You were looking around for a lock, or something holding the gate shut, but there was nothing. The gate just wouldn't open. You held up the lamp, trying to shine more light on the gate, but the rain was too heavy and thick for you to see clearly. You looked behind you. But behind you was only darkness. You then looked down at the ground—at your feet. I could feel sadness wash over you; a deep heartache. Then I woke up."

Jacob finished his recitation just as Margaret returned with two generous helpings of hot cobbler topped with vanilla ice cream. "Who had the cobbler? And who had the cobbler?" she quipped.

At the same time, Eric and Jacob said, "He did!"

"Rightie-o," Margaret said. "Enjoy, gentlemen."

Jacob took a bite and nodded with satisfaction. "Good cobbler," he said. "You've heard mine. Now tell me yours."

Eric wrapped his hands around his coffee cup, relishing the warmth. He had no need to close his eyes. His dream was crystal clear in his mind. "Same exact dream, except it was you, not me," he said. "Every detail, including the including lantern, the wind trying to un-hat you, the gate, the blinding rain. But there was one big difference. In my dream, when you pushed on the gate—it opened. You stepped through to the other side. It was after the gate shut behind you, that the sorrow came."

A shiver ran down Jacob's spine that had nothing to do with the ice cream. "What does that mean?" Jacob asked.

"I don't know. Some people interpret gates to represent security, or opportunity. Perhaps one of us is going to get an opportunity the other one doesn't share. Perhaps there safety on one side of the gate that is unavailable to the other. It feels like something for great importance is in store for one of us; something the other cannot participate in. It seems like one of us is destined to move forward, and one of us will be left behind, and both of us will be sad because of it. Whether it's you or me, remains to be seen. We'll know it when the time comes."

"Left behind?" Jacob asks. "No! I don't accept that. I *won't* accept that. God didn't call me to walk on a path ahead or behind you. We walk this path together or not at all."

Eric allowed a sad smile to cross his lips. "Thank you for that, Jacob. Believe me when I say, I wouldn't be here today if it weren't for you. I meant what I said Jacob. You saved me." Eric paused to savor his cobbler. "But life moves on. Moses led his people out of Egypt, but Joshua led them into the Promised Land. Elijah was carried into heaven in a chariot of fire, but Elisha received a double portion of the Lord's spirit. It's not for me, or you, to decide who moves forward, and who remains behind. That's in God's hands. Sometimes we are called to different paths, but it is still God who is doing the calling."

"I still don't like the idea of being left behind, any more than I like the idea of moving on and leaving you behind. Not that that is going to happen. This has always been your show. God put you in charge and I'm happy to serve in whatever capacity you need. But as far as I'm concerned, you're the one calling the shots. God's gonna have to hit me with a lightning bolt to change my mind about that."

"Perhaps," Eric said. "For now, it's a waiting game. We can't force God's hand, and why would we want to try? Just stay in the word and pray. God will reveal the meaning in His time. Trust Him for revelation. If you try to seek your own interpretation, chances are you'll only get a secular view, not God's true intention."

"I understand," Jacob said.

Silence settled over the booth while the two friend nursed their coffee and cobbler. Margaret refilled their cups, and cleared their plates.

"What are your plans for today?" Jacob asked.

"I'm going over to the school district office to sign paperwork for the location of the church service," Eric said. "I'd be lying if I said I wasn't a little nervous. You never know who you are going to encounter in these situations. Could be friend or hidden foe."

"Who's your meeting with?" Jacob asked.

"Gillian Taylor," Eric said. "She's the Superintendent of Education for Carrelton ISD."

"I think I've met her while delivering parts for district school buses. Pleasant lady; seems friendly enough."

"I have that meeting in," Eric looked at his watch, "four hours. I said it was going to be a long night. It's going to be an even longer day.

He changed the subject. "So, how are you and Renae doing?"

"Good as can be expected, I guess. It'd be better if we could figure out the whole Jesse situation. Renae worries that if she leaves him, she puts me in jeopardy—which is probably true. But sooner or later he's gonna catch us together and there'll be hell to pay. Edwards already knows we're involved, but I don't think he's told Jesse. Not yet. I'm not sure if he thinks Jesse would go off half-cocked and ruin some grand scheme of his, or if he just likes playing cat and mouse."

Jacob paused a moment in thought. "Eric, there is one thing that puzzles me."

"Only one?" the older man quipped.

Jacob smiled. "Come on. I'm serious here. For someone who doesn't believe God exists, Edwards is hell-bent on doing all in his power to destroy Him. I mean, if God doesn't exist, then what possible difference could it make to him if somebody wants to believe a lie? It would be like putting a child in jail for believing in the Tooth Fairy. Why not just point and laugh at fools lost in some delusion?"

"Ahh, the mystery of mysteries," Eric said. "I think you're right. If a person was truly an atheist, they would have no need to defend their unbelief. But I believe God put a longing in every heart, the proverbial God-shaped hole that only He can fill. People try to fill that empty space with all kinds of things; wealth, busyness, sex, booze, power is a big one. But nothing else will satisfy, and it results in bitterness. Bitterness turns to anger, envy, pride, aggression, hate. The try to tear down what they don't understand."

Eric sipped his coffee, and waved Margaret over. "Sun's about to come up. Guess it's time for breakfast. How 'bout some biscuits and gravy, and a couple of eggs, over medium. Anything for you, Jacob? My treat."

Jacob grinned. "I'll have what he's having."

Margaret nodded and hurried to greet the morning regulars who were beginning to filter in.

Would you mind going with me over to the ISD this morning?" Eric asked.

"Not a bit. I don't see how I could help though?"

"You are pretty much my right-hand man right now," Eric said looking down and tracing the rim of his cup with his finger. They both knew he meant since Will was gone. "I trust your input and admire your courage. I need that right now. When we walk together, we are stronger. *Though one may be overpowered, two can defend themselves.*"

"Just one more reason I don't accept this whole, one of us moves forward and the other is left behind, thing. There's got to be another interpretation."

Margaret shuffled to the booth and slide their plates in front of them; biscuits, eggs, and generous helpings of sausage gravy on the side. She laid the check on the table, and shuffled toward the next customer. Owner or not, she looked like she was ready to call it a night. Or a morning, as the case may be.

Jacob picked up the check, looked at it, then handed to Eric. "Your treat, remember?"

|||| |||| |||| |||| |

The predicted norther had blown through by the time they left the diner, dropping the temperature by more than 40 degrees, settling just above freezing. Jacob rubbed his hands together while waiting for Eric to unlock the car doors. The norther had carried a soaking rain with it. Eric cleared the windshield with his wipers and turned on the defroster. The sudden blast of cold air added to Jacob's discomfort.

"Gotta let her warm up a bit," Eric explained. "She runs well enough, but does take some time to get her going. I don't have the heart to get rid of her though. We've seen too much together." Eric patted the heat-stained dashboard.

"I completely understand. I've seen a lot of people with a serious devotion to their cars while delivering parts over the past few months."

Once Eric's classic was warm enough, they headed out. He drove past Roger's shop, the bank, and the local grocery store, then doubled back down the highway access roads. "Never hurts to take a circuitous route when you think someone might be following you," Eric said, his mouth a thin, grim line. Jacob nodded. He'd been check for tails as well. Eric took the turnaround and drove through a less populated area, crossing the railroad tracks to approach the ISD parking lot from the rear of the building. Satisfied they had not been followed, Eric pulled into the near-empty lot and parked on the edge under a spreading pecan tree.

Birds nesting in the tree branches greeted the rising sun with a melodic tune. Jacob thought of Renae. She loved birds. Anytime she saw one she couldn't identify, she'd pull out her *National Geographic Field Guide to the Birds of North America.* Jacob smiled, remembering her joyous "How precious" cheer once she managed to identify the critter.

Bird watching became an integral part of their dates while they were courting. They'd often sit on the side of the road or under a tree, eat a picnic lunch, and talk about life and what they wanted for the future. It was during one of those talks that Jacob, out of the blue, proposed. "Why beat around the bush, Renae. I love you. I want to spend every minute with you, accomplishing the dreams we both have. I know what I want. And that's you. What do you say? Marry me?"

Renae hadn't answered right away. She had reservations, she said. They were too young. They hadn't known each other very long. "What about…" Jacob had stopped her objections by kissing her. She found his tenacity attractive. Trusting that he knew well enough for both of them, she said "Yes." A few months later they said their I-do's in a small chapel outside of town—the cheapest place they could find.

"Jacob, you coming?" Eric said, snapping Jacob out of his reverie.

"Yeah. Sorry. Was lost in thought."

"Renae?"

"How could you tell?"

"You had that goofy look your face. I know that look. It's from a man in love, thinking about the one he loves. Seen it a million times. It might be one of the most powerful looks a man can wear. We need to go inside. I want to be in and out before anyone else knows we're here."

"Let's do this!"

The office was an open room, with desks arranged in symmetrical rows. Three were already occupied by ladies dealing with stacks of manila envelopes of varying height. Each was wrapped in a thick sweater to fight off the effects of the norther. A radio was playing hits from the 80s, and the bulletin board was littered with community notices as well as school district memos. Eric dinged the antique desk bell on the counter, and a woman with curly black hair and large round glasses raised her head and nodded. She rose from her desk and crossed to the counter with a demeanor that said, *You are imposing on my time.* Aloud she said, "What can I do for you gentleman?"

"We're here to see Gillian Taylor. Your name is?" Eric said.

"Dolores. Is she expecting you?"

"Yes, I have a nine o' clock appointment, Dolores. That is a lovely broach you have there."

Surprised, but pleased, Dolores glanced down at the silver lily broach clasped to her sweater. "What? This old thing? My daughter gave it to me for Mother's Day, just before she left home to go to college back east. I believe Gillian is in a meeting with one of the administrators. Won't you have a seat and I'll let her know you're here."

"Thank you, Dolores."

Eric and Jacob found seats along the wall and got comfortable. Eric whispered, "A person's name is the sweetest sound to them. Remembering that will get you far in life." Then he added, "It can also open doors that might not normally open for you. Also, it costs nothing to be kind."

Photos of the area sports teams were on the walls. High school varsity football. Girls' volleyball. Cross country. The high school mascot, a large Eagle. A prominent sign above the photos declared DISTRICT FOOTBALL CHAMPS 1987, 1992, 1993, 1998. Eric pointed up to the football team, "Doesn't seem to have had much success in football since the turn of the century. Did you ever play?"

"A little. I blew my knee out during my senior year. I think I could have been really good, but my grades weren't the best, and I was struggling to just get by after my parents died. That's when Jesse really proved his friendship. It wasn't just academics either. He helped me study, but he also helped me just deal with life, you know? We trained together physically; running, lifting weights. Going into my senior year, I had the chance to be really good. Second game of the season, I landed wrong stretching out for a Hail Mary. I never played another down. You?"

"I grew up in South Georgia. It's a lot like it is here in Texas. In high school, football is king. But me? I played second chair trumpet, junior and senior year."

"Mr. Lassiter," called a feminine voice.

Gillian Taylor, hugging a tan, long-sleeved jacket over her white blouse, approached. Her blond hair was pulled back in a bun. She shook Eric's hand, then turned to Jacob, her head tilted to the side, as if trying to put a name and a familiar face together.

"Jacob?"

"Yes, ma'am," Jacob replied.

"I hardly recognized you out of your shop clothes," Gillian said. "You clean up nice." She turned her attention back to Eric. "What can I do for you today?"

"Gillian, I'd like a moment of your time to talk about the abandoned gym over at Polk."

"Oh yes, we spoke on the phone. Please, follow me," Gillian directed them to a small office in the back. Her desk was cluttered with stacks of the same manila folders that adorned desks in the main office. Would you believe we still don't have all the records from Polk High digitized? It's been two years. I figured I might as well pitch in and help these girls get some of this done."

"Must be frustrating," Eric sympathized.

"It is, but that's my problem, not yours. So, what do you want to know about that musty old gym?" Gillian asked, getting to the point.

"I'd like to use it to hold a church service."

Nothing like cutting to the chase, Jacob thought.

"Gillian, I am a Pastor. My church burned down a little over a year ago, and our congregation is looking for a temporary place to hold services until we can rebuild."

"Mr. Lassiter, I'm sorry, but no can do. That building is condemned. The skylight roof was damaged during that major hailstorm last year. With the school being closed, it was never repaired and leaked with each new storm. The building is just not safe anymore. In fact, it's scheduled to be demolished next spring."

"I understand," Eric said. "Well, it was worth a shot. Thank you for your—

"But," Gillian cut him off. "What I can offer you is the choir room in building 7. It's not as big as the gym, obviously, but has decent open space, and it's still in pretty good condition. It has a better roof than the gym. Needs a good cleaning, but it's not condemned."

She opened a lower desk drawer, pulled out a form. "Just need to complete this building use request form, and make sure nobody else has a previous request to use that facility, and let's get real—the only people who have wanted to use that building since the county shut is down was a guy that wanted to do a "Haunted High School" for Halloween." She clicked her ball point pen and looked over her glasses at Eric. "Name of the responsible party?"

"Eric Lassiter."

She spoke as she wrote. "Eric Lass…" she paused. "Lassiter? That's a familiar name. I can't quite put my finger on it."

"Perhaps you remember Delanie and Elizabeth Lassiter? They attended Polk schools. Delanie would have been at the high school, and Elizabeth was about to go start Jr. high."

"There you go!" Gillian said with a sudden smile.

"Yes, I came across their names this morning while working through these files." She scanned through her finished pile and pulled out a file labeled L. "Here they are."

She pulled out two folders and flipped them open revealing school records, grades, extracurricular activities and photos of both girls. She picked them up and studied their faces. One of the girls had her hair in brown pigtails and flashed a silver toothy grin. The other had straight red hair down to her shoulders, and freckles scattered across her nose.

"Lovely girls," Gillian commented as she handed the photos to Eric.

"Yes. Yes, they were." His voice quivered as he spoke.

"Oh my god," Gillian swore as realization exploded in her memory. "They're the girls who were killed in that horrific car wreck a couple of years back. You're their father? You lost your wife in that accident as well. I'm so, so sorry!"

"Yes," Eric said, swallowing hard. "Thank you."

"I am so sorry. I didn't mean to open old wounds."

"Quite alright," Eric said, taking a breath and changing the subject, "So—the Choir room. What would the cost be to rent it out for a service, say, next Sunday?"

"Honestly, that old place has no rental value. We have to charge you something, just to comply with state formalities. How 'bout we set the rental rate at a dollar a day, and you do the cleanup? Electricity is still on, but there's no heating or air conditioning. Might not be too comfortable."

"Dollar a day sounds like something I can afford," Eric grinned. He signed the form where Gillian indicated, and she handed him a certificate of authorization to use the facility.

"That's all you need. If anyone gives you any flak or asks you what you are doing there, just show them that."

"Thank you so much, Gillian. We are forever grateful." Eric extended his hand.

She shook it. "No problem, Mr. Lassiter."

"Let's go, Jacob. Like the lady said, cleanup is our responsibility. We have a lot of work ahead of us."

As they stood to leave, Gillian said, "Mr. Lassiter, or Reverend?"

"Eric is fine with me. Pastor, if you want to be formal." He smiled.

"Pastor, is your service just your church members, or it is open to everyone? It's been a long time since I've been to church, and I'd… well, I think…"

"It's open to anyone who wants to come," Eric responded. "We would love to have you. And anyone you'd like to bring with you."

"Thank you," she said. "I might just see you next Sunday."

On their way to the car, Jacob turned to Eric, "Well, that was unexpected."

"God works in mysterious ways, His wonders to perform," Eric replied.

"I've heard that all my life," Jacob nodded. "Is that from the Psalms or Proverbs?"

"Book of Hezekiah, chapter 12, verse 6." A mischievous smile turned up the corners of Eric lips. "You should look it up when you get home."

"Thanks," Jacob said. "I will."

$$\text{卌 卌 卌 卌 II}$$

Jacob served as look-out while Eric pulled up on the campus of the old school complex. It looked much different during the day. He could see the parking enclosure they used the first night he was brought there. The auditorium was in a gated area on the right side of the campus. He and Eric had been there the night they went to the storm shelter. Jacob could see the five-barred gate as they drove past it. The gym was in the back of the complex, it too was gated. Jake could see what Gillian meant; it looked awful. He couldn't believe how much damage could occur in just two years.

"Wow, yeah, I don't think the gym would have been a good idea," said Jake.

"No, I suppose not," Eric said.

Building 7 with the choir room was on the far left side of the campus. Pulling around, he could see the **Warning: Keep Out** sign posted on the gym. Building 7 had no such sign, and no gate to block access to it. There was plenty of parking adjacent to it. The sun, high above them now, was shining off the red brick building.

"Looks old and tired," Jacob observed.

"Judge not by mere appearance," Eric responded, relating scripture to their situation.

Eric was right. While the outside was run down, the inside, though it needed work, was entirely serviceable. The choir room was a decent size; at least 50'x 50'. It was empty except for an old upright piano in the corner and some racks of folding chairs pushed up against the wall. A thick layer of dust covered everything.

"This isn't too bad," Eric said.

"If by, 'isn't too bad,' you mean, 'this is going to take a lot of work,' than I agree," Jacob said with a wry grin.

"Oh, ye of little faith," Eric said. "Frank should be on his way. Roger and Jessica won't be here until after the shop closes at five. We've got an hour or two before lunch to see what needs to be done. We need to make a to-do list, and maybe do an inventory of anything that's already here that might be useful, like the chairs and that piano. I'll start in here, why don't you check the changing rooms over there."

Jacob walked over to the door Eric pointed to and turned the knob. "Locked," he announced. "Do we have a key?"

"As long as it's the same one that fits the front door," Eric replied tossing Jacob the key.

Jacob snatched the key from the air, and inserted it into the lock. It was a tight fit, but with a little wiggle and a stiff turn, the door opened with a creak. Jacob entered a small hallway that led him to three doors. One had a sign that read, 'Ladies' another read 'Gentleman.' The third door wasn't labeled. He opened the unlabeled door to reveal the building's cleaning closet. *Pretty well stocked for a school that had been closed for two years,* Jacob thought. Along with an assortment of chemicals and paper towels, the closet housed an old Kirby vacuum cleaner. He pulled it out and wheeled it into the choir room. "What do you think about this?"

"Wow, a Kirby," Eric exclaimed. "Haven't seen one of those in years. Wonder if it still works?"

"It's a Kirby," Jacob laughed. "These things are indestructible."

"And if it doesn't, I brought a vacuum from home," Frank said as he enter the room. He tipped his hat back, put his hands on his hips, and looked around the room. "Pastor, I remember being here for Delanie's Christmas concert."

"Yes, I remember."

Their conversation was interrupted by a loud *Whrrr* coming from the old Kirby. Jacob grinned. "Well, she works," he said, turning it off and allowing the silence and dust to resettle in the room.

The three men turned their attention to the task at hand, each tackling whatever chore was in front of them, without question or complaint. A verse crossed Jacob's mind: *A cord of three strands is not easily broken.'* He thought it appropriate for a choir room, even though the word cord was spelled differently. They broke for a quick lunch of fast food burgers, then went back to work and made decent progress by the time Roger and Jessica showed up with dinner. As the evening wore on, the natural light through the windows faded rapidly into darkness. Although the electricity was on, few of the fluorescent lights in the building worked. Most of the tubes were either burned out or missing.

"I say we call it a night," Eric announced at last. "We still have a little over a week to whip this place into shape. I think first thing on the list is lighting."

"We have fluorescent tubes in stock at the hardware store," Jacob said. "Pretty sure I can get 'em at cost."

A glimmer shown in Eric's eyes. He saw the room as it was going to look—clean, renewed, filled with people praising God and loving each other. "Do you feel it? Do you feel God's presence filling this place?"

Everyone understood. It was an overwhelming sense of being part of something bigger than themselves, of being moved by a strength not their own, of being guided by a purpose beyond their comprehension. It was like getting ready for a grand finale; electric and exciting and soothing all at the same time.

The moment passed, leaving a quiet expectancy and an overriding sense of peace in its wake. Eric took one more look around the room that God had providentially led them to. And settled his gaze on the choir risers. They were pulled out into the room, creating an obstruction. They could be pushed back against the wall, one layer folding into the next. That would create more room.

"Before we leave, would you guys help me with these," he pointed at the risers. He found the release mechanism and pulled the lever. It released with a loud *clank*. "It looks like it will take most of us."

The group pushed, and one layer at a time the risers folded toward the wall and clicked into place. The railing arm that was at each end of the section folded diagonally across the four riser steps. Once the final one was in place. They all took a step back. "Well, would you look at that," Jacob said running his hand through his hair, then nodding to the wall, smiling.

"What is it?" asked Frank.

Eric nodded, understanding. "God gives us signs when we need them. We have yet another confirmation; we are in the right place."

The five sections, each folded against the wall, with the railing arm holding them into place, resembled five separate five-barred gates. Jacob explained the significance of the group. His teacher's example in the 2nd grade; the date marks on the prison wall; the one at Frank's restaurant; the broken pallet at Rogers shop; the gate entering Will's property.

"Yes, we've had that up for twenty years. Didn't realize it had such significance," Frank said.

"Funny thing is I've been meaning to get rid of that pallet for a while now. What use is a broken pallet? Now we know why I kept forgetting," Roger replied.

"Now we find it here," Eric said. "Anybody think that's a coincidence?"

"I can't see a darn thing in here," Jessica said, breaking the silence.

"Yes, we best call it a night." Eric led everyone out, shut off the lights and locked up.

"Be careful running out of here. I didn't see any goon patrol when we were coming in, but that doesn't mean they aren't out there now. No need to tip our hand too early," Roger said.

"Those flyers you wanted me to make?" Jessica said.

"Yes, have you gotten them?" Eric asked.

"Well, I was able to get the design done. Now that we have a place, I will add that. The time is still 5:00 p.m., correct?"

"Yes, that's perfect."

"I'll have that done by Friday," Jessica said. "Assuming we can get the printer fixed. It's on the fritz again."

"If not, pass it over to me or Jacob. We can see if Gillian at the School District can print them. Then on Saturday, we all can pass them out to local businesses from here to Carrelton."

As they did the first night at the shelter, they followed each other out. No headlights, as usual, until they hit the main road. Then each took a separate route home. Jacob didn't notice any sign of a tail. It was almost unnerving. For weeks they were everywhere. Now, nothing. *Perhaps that's their plan*, he thought. *To be seen, then unseen, creating a sense of paranoia. Well, it's working.*

卌 卌 卌 卌 |||

Jacob's Friday began with a call from Jessica. "Howdy, Jacob. I have the design for the flyers ready. Eric says you have a contact who can make copies? Ours over here still doesn't want to work."

"Oh yes," Jacob remembered. "Gillian Taylor. She is the superintendent at the ISD office and gave us the permit to use the choir room. I can make copies over there. I'm meeting Renae for lunch, but I can pick it up on my way to see her. I have a delivery for you anyhow."

"Sounds good. I'll be here. Later."

Jacob called Renae at the bank to double check the time for her lunch.

"Hey, Jake." He could tell from her voice that she was smiling. It made him smile. "How's your day?"

"Good. Good. Just calling to make sure you're still going to lunch at noon."

"So far, so good. Are we going to meet somewhere? Or are you picking me up?"

"Jesse still out of town?"

"Yes, he gets back tomorrow morning. Up in Austin again."

"Sounds good. Yes, I'll pick you up. But I have to run by Mills' to drop off a part and grab a flyer to take over to the ISD, so they can make copies."

"Okay. So, where are we going for lunch?"

"I was thinking Dunham's. It's close to the ISD office. I know you're pressed for time."

"Yes and no. Theresa is here today, so she can run the show while I'm gone," Renae said. "Plus, I'm the boss. If I want to take a long lunch, I can."

"You tell them, babe," Jacob said. "I'll see you soon."

Jacob loved making amends with Renae. Knowing they were getting back on track made him miss Michael even more. He wanted to see his boy, but he and Renae agreed it was the right decision to keep Michael unaware of what's going on. If the little guy unintentionally mentioned to Jesse that he saw daddy would jeopardize both of them. For now, maintaining his distance was the best course of action.

Jacob went into Stan's office, "Hey boss, I may be a little late coming back from lunch. I have to run an errand across town. The place will be closed by the time I get off, so I was hoping you'd allow me to take an extra 20 or 30 minutes? Off the clock, of course."

"I don't see that as a problem. Just make sure you get your invoicing done."

"Already there," Jacob grinned, showing him the stack he had been working on. He grabbed his jacket and headed out to pick up Renae. She was waiting for him outside the bank, wearing the peacoat he had bought her for their anniversary a couple of years ago. She loved that coat. He loved that she loved that coat.

Jacob stopped the truck in front of her, lowered the passenger window, and said, "Hey there sexy. Need a lift?"

She laughed and got in the pickup. "You're silly. How is your day?"

"Long. Invoicing. Yeesh. Makes me want to stab my eyeballs out with a fork. And yours?"

"Easy. I like being the boss," she said with a sly smile.

"You seem to be enjoying your new position a little too much," he observed.

"What can I say," she snickered. "It's good to be the king. But can we hurry. I'm starved."

"I just have to stop by Mills to get the flyer from Jessica, then to the to the ISD. Shouldn't take long. Dolores is expecting us. She's going to make us about 100 copies."

"That many? Where are you planning on putting them?"

"Local businesses. From here to Polk."

"What if Jesse or Edwards find out?"

"They are going to find out one way or another. God has protected us so far. Whatever happens now is God's will. We all agreed this service needs to take place. It's time to make our stand for Christ. Nothing can silence His word. No man, no law, no government official. Especially not one with a petty personal vendetta."

"I love it when you talk that way," Renae said. "To see you with convictions and audacity; to help instead of hurting."

"I'm sorry babe," Jacob said, pulling up to Mills Motors. He parked the car and looked into her eyes. "I truly am. I pray every night that you will somehow be able to forgive me. I have this unrelenting fear inside me that I may have hurt you so badly that you can never again fully trust me with your heart."

"I forgive you, Jake," Renae whispered. "I forgave you a long time ago. Yes, I was hurt. But I died inside when they called me and told me you were dead. I didn't want to believe it. Jesse did his best to convince, but when they wouldn't release your body to me for a service, I became skeptical. Somehow, deep down, I think I knew you were still alive. When I heard about your release, I was relieved. Jesse tried to laugh it off, like it was some kind of bureaucratic foul up. He was all, *It's water under the bridge; we're together now; you were better off thinking he was dead; just forget about him.* But I couldn't forget about you. When you called, I admit my guard was still up. Especially when I thought about the man you used to be." She took his hand and kissed it. "But you're not that man anymore. You've changed. There is a glow about you now. There is no darkness in your eyes—only light. Yes, trust is a fragile thing. But time heals, and you and I are well on our way."

"Thank you." He smiled and kissed her hand. "I'll be right back."

Jacob ran into Mills. Jessica was sitting at the front counter. "I saw that," she said. "I'm so glad the two of you are working things out. Roger and I are praying for you guys."

"Thanks. We appreciate it," Jacob said. "Is the flyer ready?"

"Here ya go." She hands him the paper. It was simple and to the point. Across the top it read 'Our Savior's Cross Reunification Service.' Below that was the date and time. Across the middle of the page was a long fence line and in the middle was a gate, a five-barred gate.

"Seems appropriate," Jacob said.

"Thought you'd like that," Jessica smiled.

"I'll drop some copies off for you on my way back. I'm taking some over to Frank to put up at Dunham's. Maybe even leave a few at the ISD for the ladies there."

Jacob hurried to the car and hopped behind the wheel. "Miss me?"

Renae laughs. "Let's go, Romeo."

Only Delores was at the ISD. Everyone else had gone to lunch. "I've been expecting you, Jacob," she said as she took the flyer. "It'll only take a moment."

"100 copies should do, Dolores." Soon he heard the clicking and swooshing of the photocopier. And a couple of minutes later she returned with a stack.

"Here you go, hot off the presses," she said. "Can I ask you a question? Is Eric Lassiter the same person who pastored Holy Cross before?"

"Yes, he is. Until…"

"It burned down." Dolores completed his sentence.

"Right. Were you a member?"

"Not regularly. But I did go there a few times. Loved his preaching," she beamed. "So, this is open to the public?"

"Everyone who wants to attend is welcome." He peeled a few copies off the top. "Here ya go. To pass around. And if you know of a good place to put one up feel free to. The more, the merrier."

"I do know of a place. Not too far from where the church used to be. I know several who attended there. I'm sure they'd be happy to know Pastor Eric is back in the saddle."

"God Bless," Jacob said. "Well, I got things to do and people to see. Hope to see you next Sunday."

"God bless you too, sweetie."

Jacob returned to the truck. "Now let's eat. I'm starving."

Jacob drove to Dunham's with a Cheshire Cat grin that had Renae asking him what was going on all the way to the restaurant. Jacob just smiled.

Once they arrived, he took Renae by the hand and led her to a booth in the back corner, already set with candles, salads, steaming rolls, two wine glasses—pitcher of iced tea.

Renae bit her lower lip to keep from giggling at the unexpected romantic gesture, then did actually giggle when he pour her a glass of tea?

"We both still have work to go back to," he explained. "It would set a bad example for the boss-lady to have alcohol on her breath."

"When did you plan this out?"

"This morning," he grinned, enjoying the glow on Renae's face. "I called Frank up and told him I needed a quick lunch. Grilled salmon and dirty rice. Am I right?"

She smiled the way he loved—tucking her chin down and closing her eyes. "You remember."

"I might have been a jerk in the old days, but I wasn't a complete jerk. I still remember several things that made you fall in love with me."

They finished their salads just as the entrée arrived. They talked about old times; about picnic lunches on the ranch, and late nights staring at the stars and dreaming about the future. They talked about Michael and how much he's grown. They talked about the ordeal facing them, and prayed it would be over soon.

"Maybe after the service we can come out in the open, confront Jesse about his part in the whole coverup, and get our life back again," Jacob said.

Renae nodded, a shy smile playing with the corners of her mouth. "I'd like that," she said. "I'd like for you to come home."

The meal passed far too quickly. He dropped Renae off just in time to get a few flyers to Jessica, and left a stack there for Eric, who was coming by their shop later. He made a couple of stops at convenience stores and shops around the hardware store.

Well, we wanted things out in the open. No turning back now. Back at the hardware store, he even managed to get Stan's permission to put a couple of flyer's in the window and set a small stack by the register.

Before the hour was over the got a text from Eric. *It's all in God's hands now. Lord help us!*

ꟼꟼꟼꟼꟼ

Jacob padded down the hall in his pajama bottoms heading toward the pounding on his front door. He looked through the peephole and saw a hand holding one of his flyers.

"Open up Jake," Jesse's voice was intense. "We need to talk about this."

Jacob unlocked, but leaves the chain latched. "It's late, Jesse. What can I do for you?"

"You can let me in for starters. C'mon Jacob. I'm your friend, remember? I'm not here to hurt you. I just want to know what's going on."

Jesse looked like a whipped dog. He had a downtrodden slouch, even in his starched, white uniform. Jacob paused for a moment and said a silent prayer. He felt no check in his spirit, so he nodded, slid the chain, and opened the door. "Come on in before you wake the neighbors."

Jesse slunk into the room, plopped down on the couch, and slapped the flyer on the coffee table. "Why Jacob? Haven't you suffered enough? Why do you insist on poking the bear. This ridiculous stunt is only going to tick Edwards off. You know that, right?"

"You mean the service? It's not a stunt. It's just a church service."

"*Just* a church service? And Adolf Hitler was *just* a corporal. You know what Edwards is capable of. He'll put you in the ground over this. He thought sending you a message with the fire was enough. As long as you kept your little meetings confined to Mills Motors—"

"Mill's Motors?" Jacob interrupted.

"Of course Mill's Motors. You think he didn't know? As long as you were meeting in secret, just a few of you, not stirring up trouble or causing anyone any discomfort, he was fine. I think he might have even enjoyed toying with you, playing a little game of cat and mouse. What harm could you do? And he was free to fry bigger fish. But this?" He pointed at the flyer. "When he sees this all hell will break loose, and there will be nothing I can do to stop it. Why, Jake? Why did you have to do this now, just when everything was starting to settle down?"

"Jesse," Jacob paused, trying phrase his response in a way his friend would understand. "This is not something we set out to do. It's not some big statement against the government, and we're certainly not trying to thumb our noses at Edwards. Believe me, I've seen the inside of his prison and I have no desire to spend even one more night there. But this is beyond me. It's beyond Eric and any of the others. This was orchestrated by God. We're just following the path He has set our feet on."

"Jesus Christ, Jake."

"Jesus Christ is right, Jesse," Jacob said with holy reverence. "He's the whole point of this service."

"I don't get it, Jake. The guy I knew didn't even believe in God."

"The guy you knew is dead, Jesse," Jacob said. "In a way, when you told Renae I died in prison, you were right. The old Jacob did die, and the new Jacob was born. Or, at least, I was born again.

"Jesse, I'm serious. This isn't just some religious mumbo-jumbo or double talk. I'm telling you what happened to me in that prison. I hit rock bottom. When you're all alone in an 8 by 10 cell with nothing to distract you, you get to know yourself pretty good. I was confronted by the person I was, and I didn't like that guy very much. That guy didn't know much beyond his own pain and anger, and the only way he knew to communicate was by causing more pain and anger in others. I hurt people, Jesse. A lot of people. With my words. Not the least of which was you. I don't blame you for hating me and wanting me to suffer. I deserved it."

Jesse stood up and paced the room. He stopped at the window and peeked out. "I don't hate you, Jake. I never have."

"Wait. What?"

Jesse turned to face him. "I never hated you, but I did envy you. You always seemed to have something I wanted, but couldn't seem to grasp. Renae, for one. And now this, this—whatever this thing is that has made you different."

"What's made me different is forgiveness," Jacob said. "I've been forgiven. I feel clean. I am whole again. I feel as strongly about this as I have felt about anything. That's what this church service is about, Jesse.

"We're not trying to create any kind of movement, and we're not trying to be a burr under Edwards' saddle. But the time for meeting in secret is over. People need to hear the simple truth that God loves them, and gave His one and only son, Jesus Christ, so that they could be born again.

"Jesse, the truth is, the Gospel is offensive to those who don't receive it. Jesus said the world would hate Him, and if it hated Him it would hate His followers. But the Gospel is Good News. And it is true. So, we're going to have a church service and invite anyone who wants to come. If Official Edwards feels he needs to do something about it, we understand. If he comes with guns blazing, we don't fear the one who can kill the body but not the soul. No more cowering in a dirty shop. No more secret meetings. We will stand in the light and shout it from the rooftops that Jesus is Lord. No law made by man can stop us. Edwards can't stop us. And with all due respect, you can't stop us either."

The room was completely still for a long moment. Jesse broke the silence. "Who says I want to?"

"Jesse, you do what you have to do," Jacob said. "I know you have a job to do, so whatever that is, do it. I will not hold it against you. I'm in God's hands now."

"I've never heard you speak this way," Jesse said. "What happened to you?"

"Lord God in heaven," Jacob laughed. "How many ways do I have to say it? I've been saved. I've been born again. I found Jesus—or better yet, Jesus found me. I'm a new creation is Christ. Don't you get it? God loves you! And what happened to me, can happen in you too. Christ died for everyone. And anyone can come to Him for forgiveness and receive it. If you believe it, and allow it to change you inside, then you can experience the wholeness I have been telling you about."

Jesse just shook his head and returned to the couch and collapsed on it, as if he were exhausted. He reached into his shirt pocket, and pulled out a lined piece of paper. He held it up. "Do you know what this is?"

"Christmas list?" Jacob quipped.

"For you, maybe," Jesse sighed. "It's a letter from Renae. She says that she can't live with me anymore. She knows my secret and we're finished. She says she is taking Michael and they are going to stay at her parents until I have the opportunity to move out."

"Is that right?" Jacob feigned surprise.

"Anyone ever told you, you have a terrible poker face."

A sheepish grin creased Jacob's face. "Okay, I may have seen Renae a time or two since I got out."

"A couple of times," Jesse barked a wry laugh. He held up his hand. "It's alright. I'm not upset. Truth is I never wanted to come between you and Renae. Don't get me wrong, she's a great girl, but not really my type. That was all at Edwards instigation. He has a way of getting what he wants from people, especially people who work for him."

Jacob's jaw dropped. He tried to talk, but he couldn't formulate any words to respond to that bombshell.

"Anyhow, Renae loves you, Jacob. Don't ever doubt that. She never gave up. Even when I moved in, she would not shut up talking about you. Yeah, she didn't like the man you had become, the guy who shot off his mouth so often it landed him in prison, but she never stopped loving you. Even when I tried to convince her that you were dead, all she would say was, *No body, No death*. She's a tenacious woman, bro. Hope you know what you're getting yourself into.

"And let me get this out of the way, because I know your wondering—we never slept together. Not gonna lie, I tried. I mean, she's—well, you know, she's your wife. But she was never comfortable with it, and I'm not a guy that pushes myself on a woman. I played it off like I was willing to be with her and comfort her until she was ready, but the truth is, she was never going to be ready."

The room went quiet again, both men letting what was said sink in.

Jesse continued, "You know, Edwards actually liked you. You were a challenge. He loves finding people who are a lot like him, then bending them to his will. That's what he considers a great triumph. But this," he pointed at the flyer, "this is final straw. He believes if you can't be bent, you'll have to be broken. It's likely to get ugly."

"Jesse, I'm sorry," Jacob said.

"For what?" Jesse laughed. "For telling me the truth? Even back in the old days when you were being a giant prick, you were right. I'm shallow. I don't care about anything but myself and how the situation is going to benefit me. Everything you said that made me despise you and end our friendship was spot on. I hated you because you were right.

"Working with Edwards has its perks—prestige, power, and the money, oh Jacob, the money. I don't know what branch of government we work for, but it is well-funded. I mean, you saw the Denali. The expense account is bottomless; *any means necessary* includes at any expense necessary."

"You can just quit Jesse. Quit and get away from it all."

Jesse shook his head with a sad smile. "I can't quit. You don't know these people. They have their claws in me so deep, there is no way out. I just have to keep on doing what I am doing. But I gotta say, Jacob, you've made it hard. You aren't the man I despise anymore. I no longer want to hurt you—or Renae. Honestly, it's Edwards I despise now, for putting me in this position. And I despise myself for allowing him to put me in this position."

"So what happens now?"

"If Edwards hasn't already seen your flyers, he'll hear about them soon enough. Once that happens he'll call a meeting of his staff to figure out the best way to put a stop to it, legally.

I'll try to convince him the best course of action is to do nothing, that the meeting won't amount to anything, that nobody will show up and your little church will die on the vine. I'll suggest we monitor the situation, note who attends and pay them a friendly visit, just so they know the consequences of their actions. That's the best I can do."

"That's more than I can ask, Jesse," Jacob said. "But if I know Edwards, he'll send a few moles in to take notes of any illegal utterances from the pulpit."

"That's likely," Jesse agreed. "If your buddy the preacher says anything resembling what he said in Atlanta, game over. I guarantee you Edwards will have him arrested. Most likely you too, since you didn't go down like he expected. I don't think you have to worry much about Dunham or the Mills couple; they're small potatoes as far as Edwards is concerned. Cut off the head and the body dies, as the saying goes."

"I understand, Jesse. Honestly, I have no idea what kind of sermon Eric will preach, but whatever it is, we're fully expecting trouble. But we also fully expect God to do wonders through this service. If He chooses to save us from Edwards, great! If not, and it's back to prison, we're ready to take the consequences of living out our faith."

"You always were a stubborn cuss," Jesse said, a hint of admiration in his tone. "I'll do my best to prevent trouble before your service. I cannot guarantee what will happen after."

Jesse's phone rang, and he pulled it from his pocket, looked at caller ID, and showed it to Jacob. "Speak of the devil," he said.

"Jesse, haul your butt to the office, now," Edward barked into the phone loud enough for Jacob to hear it without the speaker turned on. "They are planning something big, and we need to head it off!"

"On my way, chief." Jesse clicked the phone off, then fixed Jacob with a warning stare. "I hope you know what you are doing." He started for the door, then stopped and shook Jacob's hand. "For whatever it's worth, Jake, I forgive you. And I ask you to forgive me—not just for all the stuff I've done, but for what I'm likely to do on Sunday."

"Do your job, Jesse," Jacob said, pulling him into a hug. "It's in God's hands."

Jesse nodded, then left, pulling the door closed behind him. Jacob watch through the peep hole as his old friend walked to his company-issued Denali and drove away into the night.

"Is he gone?" Renae asked, stepping up behind him.

"Yes."

"Do you think he knew I was here?"

"I don't know. Does it matter?"

She put her arms around his waist and pressed herself into his back, kissing his neck. "You okay?"

"I guess so. I just—feel sorry for him, you know? I feel like somehow this is all my fault."

"Jesse has always been Jesse. He made his own decisions. He said it himself, all he ever really cared about was himself and how things affected him. You can't blame yourself for his choices. Those were always his to make."

"I guess you're right." He turned around and embraced his wife. "I love you, Renae. I'm afraid things are going to get ugly. I really believe Jesse will do what he can, but if push comes to shove, his loyalties lie with himself, and that means ultimately he'll support Edwards. Maybe you *should* go up to your parents. Just to be safe."

"My place is here. If you're going to fight this, I'm going to fight it with you. I'll stay here until Jesse moves out. Then we all, as a family, will move back home. Now, it's late. We should go back to bed."

A soft whine came from bedroom as Michael stirred.

"You want to go check on him?" Renae asked.

"I would love to." Jacob kissed her on the forehead and went to check on his son.

$$\text{卌 卌 卌 卌 卌}$$

The week flew by faster expected with no interference from Edwards or anyone in a Denali. Maybe Jesse had been true to his word. Maybe Jesse would warn them of Edwards' plans. Maybe not. They would have to wait until Sunday to find out. Either way, the anticipation was building. There was an electricity in the air, like static before an impending thunderstorm.

Jacob and Renae, Eric and the Mills successfully placed their flyers in many of the businesses around Carrelton and Polk, and most of the reaction was positive. Some sniffed that there were plenty of churches in town if someone wanted to go. Why would anyone attend a service in an old, run-down, condemned school building. Eric always responded with a question: "Did the laws affect the way your preacher preaches?" Most admitted they had. It was rare these days to hear about sin, or repentance, or the need for a savior.

"We plan to change that," Eric explained, and while a few laughed, or shook their heads in warning, many said, "It's about time." It gave them hope of a good turnout, but they also knew nothing they said would draw the people. That was God's responsibility. "We extend an invitation, but the Holy Spirit does the drawing," Eric was fond of saying.

Renae grew in admiration for the man Jacob had become, especially with the way he handled rejection. The old Jacob would have lashed out, like a little kid trying to win an insult battle. Now, while she could still see the fire burning on the inside, he'd grin, nod, and walk away without a word other than, "Thank you for your time. God Bless you."

When Saturday night rolled around, the core group, which included Renae, gathered in the storm shelter for one last prayer meeting. The choir room was cleaned and arranged. The lighting had been repaired, and the atmosphere was set with plants and flowers throughout the room. They set up a makeshift platform directly in front of the group of five-barred gates, using them as a backdrop. It was all centered around the podium that once stood at the front of the shelter meeting room.

Three chairs were set up to the right of the podium with music stands in front of them. Frank had talked a couple of his college buddies into playing with him. One played the fiddle and the other a bass.

The chairs were arranged in neat rows, and a fold-out table from the storage room was placed near the entrance where it served as a welcome center, complete with bulletins, a sign-in sheet, and handouts of Eric's story.

It all now boiled down to a prayer meeting in a storm shelter 150 feet below the surface. As their hands joined, a sense of awe fell on them. The atmosphere felt—heavy, was the only way Jacob could describe it. Not oppressive, but thick with importance, with reverence, and power. Fear ceased to exist, or if it did, it appeared as a distant memory, a thing to insignificant to trifle with. The more they prayed and pressed into the moving of the Holy Spirit, the greater their confidence in the sovereign work of God grew. Jacob became aware of Eric speaking in a voice filled with authority like he had never heard before.

"No one and no thing can stop what is about to happen. No level of hatred, no amount of opposition, no evil plot of the adversary will prevent the work of God from continuing. No weapon formed against us will stand.

"Lord, keep our eyes focused on You. Keep our minds fixed on You. Use my words for Your glory. Guide our worship for Your honor. Take us into Your presence, for Yours is the kingdom, and the power, and the glory, forever! Amen."

Silence reigned for a long moment, no one willing to disturb the holiness of the experience. At last Jacob said in hushed tones, "I know all of you have experienced things like this before. Me, I've never allowed the opportunity to present itself. Before I met Eric, and each of you, I shunned God. I was prideful. I felt I was better than anyone, that I certainly wasn't so weak that I needed God. But I was wrong. True weakness is thinking you don't need God. Thank you for accepting me. Thank you for showing me how much God means to you, so I can find out how much He means to me."

"You are not the only one who has learned something here Jacob," Eric said. "We have learned that God still changes hearts. We get so bogged down by *experiencing* God that we fail to notice that God wants to change people's lives. Sometimes we get so focused on our own relationship with God that we forget the fields are white for the harvest. There are so many souls dying to hear the Word. We just have to tell them."

It was nearly 10:00 p.m. when they ended the meeting. They felt no need to file secretly out of the parking lot. Everyone drove with their lights on. The secret was out, the battle lines were drawn, and there was no need to hide anymore.

Jacob and Renae drove in silence for a while, allowing the

residue of the evening's meeting to permeate the atmosphere of the truck. "I can see what you are talking about now with Pastor Eric," Renae said. "What an amazing man of God. I'm grateful you met him."

"I am too," Jacob said. He adjusted the rearview mirror to see Michael asleep in his car seat holding tight to a stuffed bear. He thought of Jesse's warning, and a frown crossed his face momentarily, then vanished like a vapor. Tomorrow could take care of tomorrow's troubles. Tonight, he was a happy man.

IIII IIII IIII IIII IIII I

Renae drove back to her home that night. Jacob wanted to go with her, but Renae vetoed the idea. Jesse had moved out, but she wanted the chance to clean the house, to remove any evidence of another man having lived there. She wanted to bring Jacob back to the home he remembered.

"I don't care," Jacob had insisted.

"But I do." Renae crossed her arms across her chest in the universal feminine stance that said *argument is futile*, so Jacob did the intelligent thing and relented.

Jacob was afraid he wouldn't sleep at all that night. He remembered seeing the clock click over to 2:00 a.m., and the next thing he remembered was waking up to the birds chirping outside his window. Manic energy took over again, with his mind moving faster than his body could react. *The Spanish have a word for what I'm feeling,* he thought. *Ancias. It's the chills you get when you are anxious about something.*

He gave Renae a quick call. "You up?"

"Yeah. Finally," she mumbled. "Had a difficult time sleeping last night."

"I feel your pain," Jacob empathized.

"It wasn't as easy as I thought coming back here," she said. "I just need to grab a few things for Michael's bag, and we're on our way."

"Okay, see you at the church."

Jacob's *ancias* resulted in leadfoot syndrome, because he arrived at Polk far more quickly than he anticipated. But his enthusiasm was challenged as he cruised into the parking lot. Three Denali's were lined up toward the back of the school, parked on the outskirts with their motors running, exhaust vapors punctuating the crisp morning air: Edwards white Denali, the deputy's silver, and Jesse's black one.

Jacob wasn't afraid, but he was cautious. *Greater is He who is with us than he who is against us*, he quoted to himself.

Eric was already inside. His Buick, trunk open was backed into a spot up front. Jacob parked next to the Buick, hopped out, and looked at the boxes of hymnals in the trunk. He grabbed one and headed into the sanctuary, meeting Eric who was making a return trip. "Morning, Pastor. I assume these are going inside?"

"Yes, sir, they are. How are you this morning Jacob?"

"Blessed. Excited. Exhausted. I don't know how to explain it."

Eric laughed. "Yes, sir, that's the human reaction to the Holy Spirit on the verge of something powerful." Eric nodded over to the Denali's. "I guess you saw our audience. Where's Renae?"

"She's on her way. She had to stop by the house to pick up some things for Michael. And yes, I saw our company," Jacob said. "You know, I'm not afraid of them anymore. I'll admit driving up onto the three of them, my heart skipped a beat, but it didn't freeze like it normally does. It even made me laugh a bit."

"That's the peace that passes understanding," Eric said as he grabbed another box from his trunk.

Jacob set his box down in what was once a choir room,

but was now a sanctuary. He closed his eyes and took a deep breath. The musty smell that once filled this place was replaced with the smell of jasmine and fresh flowers. He opened his eyes took in his surroundings—a room filled with empty seats—and unlimited potential.

"What?" Eric asked as he set his box next to the other two.

Jacob, lost in the moment, didn't even see him walk in. "Nothing. Something. I don't know. You know that feeling you get on a roller coaster as you are climbing? The clicking and clanking of the chains pulling you up the steep incline. Your heart is beating in tandem with each click and clank. Then you reach the top, and you can see the entire park; you're alone with just your heartbeat and the breeze, right before you head stomach first toward the earth below. That feeling? Yeah, that about sums it up. I'm right at the top."

"You ready for it?" Eric asked, placing his hand on Jacob's shoulder.

"For what?"

"The sudden plummet back to earth; the ride my friend," Eric said with a smile and a slap on the back.

"Let's do this," Jacob said, raising both hands in the air, "Wheeeee!!"

"Amen, brother!" Roger said as he entered with the final box of hymnals.

"I've never felt so alive," Jacob said.

"Holy Ghost power," Roger replied.

"Hey Pastor, where do you want this set up?" Jessica asked. She was carrying a box with a couple of coffee dispensers.

"Over near that storage closet. There are plugs over there. How many did you bring?"

"Four. I figured three regular and one decaf."

"That'll work. There is a table up against the wall over there. Inside the closet on a shelf, you'll find a stack of napkins. You know Margaret, right?"

Jessica nodded. "Who doesn't?"

"Right," Eric smiled. "Well, I was able to convince Maggie's to bring 12 dozen doughnuts. They should be here shortly."

"That's wonderful," Jessica said. "I'll get those tables set up and the coffee brewing." She turned to Jacob. "Where's Renae?"

"She'll be here in a bit. Needed things for Michael at the house."

"Looking forward to seeing her," Jessica said, then headed over to the closet.

Everyone was working on something. The flow that permeated the air and the beat of Southern gospel tunes on the sound system set a rhythm to work by. By the time Frank and his band arrived the scent of coffee was dancing with the smell of jasmine, every chair had a hymnal with a box left over, and Margaret and her husband James were unloading the final tray of freshly baked doughnuts adding to the commingled aromas.

Frank introduced the rest of his band, each one was a little bit older than the other. The three set up and plugged into the sound system. Eric pointed to it and explained, "Had that thing in an extra room we have at the house. We used it for a park ministry we had in Atlanta. On Saturdays, during the summer we would go out to the neighborhood park and hold a small service. The church youth group would perform drama skits, we'd sing a few recognizable songs, and I'd give a brief sermonette." He smiled, looking at the floor as the memories grabbed him. "Good times."

"This should be pretty exciting then," Jacob said.

Frank announced they were ready with a strum of his guitar. It reverberated through the room giving a small feedback squelch through the speakers. "Sorry." He walked over to the soundboard and twisted a knob. He gave it another strum, this one nice and crisp. "Billy Jr. should be here in a second with a couple more microphones."

"Billy Jr.?" Jacob asked.

"Will's son," Eric said.

"Oh wow," Jacob said. "I didn't know."

"Estranged. Will and his wife separated shortly after I arrived from Atlanta. She filed for divorce after he began helping me out."

Jacob always wondered why Will never really gave him much advice about his and Renae's marriage. Now he knew.

Jacob went out to move his car to give the front spaces for others. He parked over near the covered carport where they would hide their cars for the storm shelter. Eric was already walking back after moving his car as well. He could see Renae pulling into the lot. She saw him too and drove over to where he was. *This should be interesting.* They parked side by side. Renae lifted Michael from his car seat and the toddler spotted his dad.

"Daddy!" Michael ran to him and gave him a big hug.

"I missed you, bub," Jacob said.

"Me too daddy. I'm hungry."

"You just ate sweetie," Renae explained.

"I know, but I'm still hungry. Do you have food, Daddy?"

Jacob laughed. "Yes, I have a doughnut for you inside."

"Ooh, I love doughnuts," Michael said with a bounce.

"Come on; let's go inside." Jacob picked up his son and carried him.

Renae walked along side Jacob, taking his free hand in hers. She nodded toward the Denalis. "He been there long?"

"All morning. You don't have to hold my hand if it makes you uncomfortable."

She chuckled. "Not in the least, my love."

Eric, who was now placing signs pointing the way to the repurposed choir room, called out, "Hello, Renae." Eric dusted off his hands and crossed to me the newly reunited family. He shook her hand and turned to Michael. "Well Howdy there, little buckaroo."

"Howdy," Michael said. "Who are you?"

They all laughed. "This is Pastor Eric," Jacob explained.

"Howdy, Pastor Eric," Michael said.

"Good to have you here Renae. I am blessed to see your family together."

"Thank you, Pastor," Renae said. "If it weren't for you, none of this would be happening."

"No, if it weren't for the Lord," he grinned. "I am just the instrument he used to help you to realize God's plan."

"Well then, thank the Lord."

"Go on inside. I think Jessica is waiting for you," Eric said. "Jacob, can you help me with the rest of these signs?"

"Certainly," Jacob put Michael down and patted him on the behind. "Go help Mommy inside. I'll be there in a minute."

"He looks just like you," Eric said, watching the two of them head inside. "You are blessed, Jacob. Don't ever take that for granted."

"I did once," Jacob acknowledged. "Never again. So, how can I help?"

"There nothing left to do. I just wanted to talk to you

privately before things get too busy. I'll be brief. You know things are liable to get crazy, right?"

"Yes, I guess I have given it some thought."

"The men in those cars are here to do one thing and one thing only. They don't care if this parking lot is packed and cars line the highway waiting to get in. I think Edwards would probably prefer it that way; more witnesses makes a bigger example. They are here to catch us violating the law by saying something they construe to being offensive, so they can take us both back to prison. I'm going to preach the word of God, so chances are, by the end of this day, I won't be a free man."

"I'm right here with you Eric. I'll go with you. Happily."

"I don't want that. I need you out here to keep things going when I'm gone," Eric said. "You have a family to think of. Mine is long gone. There is only me now. You just had your marriage restored, and I have to tell you—Renae is a gift from Heaven—and Michael knows your face and calls you Daddy. Remember, take nothing for granted. I understand your devotion to me and to this whole thing we've started. But our paths go down different roads. Remember those dreams. Your path continues from today. Mine ends.

"Most likely he won't try anything until the service is over. Knowing how meticulous he is, he wants the whole thing documented. From start to end. There will likely be two or three informants in our congregation today. To build a good case against me, he will want the entire service to take place. He's here now for intimidation, just to see if I'll really go through with it. But make no mistake, he's coming.

"Please don't try to find out who his plants are. That would put you in a position of getting arrested again. Do not prejudge anyone. The word of the Lord can penetrate even the hardest of hearts. Who knows, the people he sent to trap me, might end up getting saved. Wouldn't that be a great plot twist. It worked with Paul. So, focus on reflecting Christ. Extend compassion to everyone. God will do the rest."

"So, when Edwards makes his move, you want me to stand silent and do nothing?" asked Jacob with disapproval.

"That's exactly what I want you to do," Eric said. "Cooperate completely."

"I don't know if I can do that, Eric. I don't want to see you go back to prison. Not alone."

"Jacob, you have no choice. I know that now. And I am okay with it. Someone needs to take a stand. That someone is me. That's God's call on my life."

"And I will do what I feel I have to do."

"I understand, and I would never tell you to disobey the Holy Spirit. But you also have to consider the ramifications. Is going back to jail in the best interest of your family?" Eric asked. "Yes, it is God first, always. But your family comes in a close second. Don't put me or this movement before Renae and Michael. Besides, I need you free to continue out here. You do no good if you are put away with me. I need your word, Jacob. Do nothing. Cooperate. Jacob, your word?" Eric stuck out his hand.

Jacob looked at Eric's hand, looked over to the Denali's then back into Eric's eyes. His dark brown eyes pierced his heart. Jacob knew he had to do what he had to do. He grabbed hold of it, "I give you my word, Pastor."

"Let's get this show on the road. Many have already arrived."

Eric and Jacob shook many hands while walking back into the church. Cars continued to pour into the lot. People from all over the region. They recognized people they met on their invitation trek across the towns—people from Carrelton, Prairietown, Brighton, and locally in Polk.

One by one they saw the ladies from the ISD, including Gillian Taylor, who gave an enthusiastic wave to Jacob. Stan and Giselle from Jacob's work; a few of the tellers from the bank where Renae worked. Margaret and her husband, who stayed after the doughnut delivery, said they knew of dozens that were coming out. It had been the buzz around the restaurant for the last couple of days.

The Heavenly Trio was filling the sanctuary with beautiful music, bluegrass style. The acoustics within the converted choir room was perfect for music. People were talking and meeting new friends. Roger was glad-handing some of the guys from the feed store in Brighton and introducing them to the men who worked the stockyard in Prairietown. Renae and Jessica made sure the doughnut plates stayed full, and coffee canisters remained stocked. Margaret helped dispense the coffee while still calling everyone *sweetie* or *darling*. *You can take the waitress out of the restaurant…* Jacob laughed. He continued around the room, introducing himself, making new acquaintances, and meeting new family.

The room grew full. Eric's premonition of a full parking lot with little room to spare was coming to pass. Jacob tried to count heads, but kept losing track. Not that numbers mattered. Numbers were just numbers. It was the people that counted.

It was close to 10:00 when Jacob heard the pop of the microphone being turned on. Frank announced, "Can everyone please find a seat? We will begin shortly. We praise God that you came out to be with us today. Grab a doughnut while they last and a hot cup of coffee. We want to thank Millie's over on 37 for the delicacies. Again, we will start shortly."

Frank went back to his guitar and gave a look over at Billy Jr, a spitting image of his father minus the beard. Frank strummed his guitar. No feedback this time. He looked to Bud and Jerry and began to bounce his head in time. They played a couple of songs Jacob didn't know. But they made him want to jump up and dance in the middle of the room.

A couple more people came up to him and thanked him for the invitation. They were excited to be there. Jacob made his way to the front row where Renae and Michael were sitting, and nestled in beside them.

"You ready for this?" Renae leaned into him and asked.

"Ready as I'll ever be." Jacob said.

HHT HHT HHT HHT HHT ||

The second song ended, and a sense of hushed reverence pervaded the room. Silence reigned as worshippers soaked in the presence of the Holy Spirit. When the moment was right, Eric walked to the podium and addressed the congregation. "Thank you, everyone, for coming out. I'm so blessed to see each one of you. Please, have a seat. We have a lot planned for today. I trust you have had the opportunity to get acquainted with old friends, or even make a new one or two.

"In case I haven't made my way around to you, let me introduce myself. I am Pastor Eric Lassiter. I was the pastor of Our Savior's Cross Baptist Church here in Polk, up until a little over a year ago when a fire destroyed our building. I was away for a while, but as you can see, I'm back. I see several folks here who were part of that congregation. Thank you for being here.

"I had plenty of time to press into my relationship with God over the past year, and I've met some strong people in the faith; people who helped bring me out of the discouragement I found myself in. God is good! Amen?"

"Amen," sounded throughout the crowd.

"I'd like to take a moment to recognize a few of those individuals. You don't have to come up here; just stand up and wave as I call you. Roger and Jessica Mills. They own Mills Motors over in Carrelton. This morning you probably saw her over at the coffee setup with Margaret, who every-one knows from Maggie's. You have had the pleasure of listening to Frank Dunham and the Heavenly Trio during the pre-service. He owns the restaurant over on Highway 16 between Carrelton and Brighton.

"This last month has been tough on all of us here. We lost a good friend and brother in Christ, William Johnson. But we have the next best thing. His son, Billy Jr. is here running the sound system for us.

"There is one man I want to thank especially. While I was away, I almost gave up on God. I was in a pit so deep I had to look up to see bottom. God used him and his passions to keep me from closing the door completely. Jacob Andrews, please stand."

A round of applause arose. Reluctant, Jacob stood, gave a small wave, and quickly sat back down. Renae beamed with pride and squeezed his hand.

"Thank you, Jacob. If it weren't for your tenacity, none of this could have happened. Thank you, brother," Eric said. "Ok, now. Who's ready to worship? Let's welcome The Heavenly Trio."

"Howdy everyone," Frank started. "Everyone should have a hymnal underneath their seat if they'd like to follow along. Otherwise, the lyrics are printed out in the bulletin I trust you grabbed as you entered. Let's worship the Lord. "How Great Thou Art" is 293 in your hymnal."

Frank led the congregation through rousing call to worship song, upbeat praise, and into songs of worship and adoration, before turning the service back to Eric. The applause died down, Eric picked up his Bible, pulled his glasses from his pocket and put them on, then instructed the faithful, "If you have your Bibles, please turn to the book of Matthew. We will be reading the seventh chapter, verse 13 and 14:

"Enter through the narrow gate. For wide is the gate and broad is the road that leads to destruction, and many enter through it. But small is the gate and narrow the road that leads to life, and only a few find it."

Eric prayed, both aloud and silently, seeking wisdom and courage to speak the words the Lord had given him for such a time as this.

Eric paused for a long moment and gazed out over the congregation, making eye contact with many of the attendees. He smiled, turned his back on the audience, and looked at the risers behind him, with their symbolic five-barred gates. Then turning back to face his congregation, he said, "If you look behind me you will see something extraordinary that you may not have noticed before.

"I think that's the way it is with most things in life. We see the ordinary, and every once in a while God pulls back the curtain and allows us to see the spiritual truth behind the ordinary. As many of you probably know, this room was once the choir room for the high school. But behind that ordinary, God was preparing a sanctuary for the preaching of His word.

"Look at the risers folded up behind me. They're just risers, the kind you likely seen hundreds of times if you happened to go to high school." There was a smattering of laughter from the congregation. "But look a little closer. Use your spiritual eyes, if you will. Do you see it? Do you notice what these folded up risers resemble? If you live out in the country, or even just driven through it, you most likely have seen a five-barred gate. Behind me stands five of them.

"Some of you are cattlemen. You understand the difference between a wide and narrow gate. Try to herd cattle through a narrow gate is difficult. Cattle don't like narrow gates. They are far more comfortable moving through a wide gate. I think most people are like cattle. We prefer the wide gate. It's easier to move through.

"Another thing about cattle—they tend follow the cow in front of them. You've probably heard the old saying, 'If you ain't the lead bull, the view never changes.'" Another smattering of laughter. "Well, that's true. People tend to follow people without much thought of venturing out on their own. The wide path is comfortable. The wide path has been worn smooth by the tramping of generations of feet for millennia. And of course there is safety in numbers, right?"

"The narrow path, the straight gate—it can certainly look like a more difficult journey. Not a lot of people take it. It doesn't look comfortable. It may lead through wilderness, or along rocky paths, up into the mountains, or down into valleys, even into what appears to be the valley of death. It may be dangerous. It may be lonely. People tend to shy away from dangerous, and lonely, and uncomfortable. But let me tell you, friends. That wide path that all the cattle are following, one after another, leads to the slaughterhouse, and all those cows end up as a steak on a platter at Dunham's Restaurant, or a hamburger at Maggie's.

"In the natural, the wide path looks like the way to go. But if you pull back the curtain, if you gaze through spiritual eyes, you'll see that there is a way that appears right to a man, but the end thereof is death. People are not cattle, but we are all on a journey, and we all choose the path we walk. The wide path includes embracing the popular opinion of the culture, or following the politically correct way of doing things. Popular opinion tells you there many roads leading to God. Popular opinion tells you that you *should* be comfortable. Popular opinion says if it feels good, do it. But friends, popular opinions and political correctness never has and never will lead to life. Following the herd leads to death and destruction. It always has, and it always will.

"Thank God there is another path. It's narrow. It's scary. It requires trust and faith. It might lead you to the very edge. Oh, but friend, the best views are always from the edge! The narrow path, the one that leads to the narrow gate, that's the one that leads to life." Eric paused, and a tinge of sadness entered his voice as he announce, "An unfortunately the word of God tells us that there are few who find it.

"The truth is, you can enjoy the pleasures of sin for a season. But happiness, *true* happiness, happiness that abides beyond a season, that extends throughout your lifetime and on into eternity can only be found in the Lord. The narrow path is the path to joy, and joy is not dependent upon your circumstances. Joy is not dependent on feeling. Does your job irritate you? Joy says, 'At least you have the opportunity to make a living.' Does your life seem to be going nowhere? Joy says, 'Breathe in, breathe out. You're still alive.' Do you wake up next to your spouse and just wonder, why? Well, joy says, "Hey, at least someone was brave enough to marry you."

A murmur of laughter rippled through the crowd.

Eric leaned over the podium, looked over his glasses, and declared, "Joy is about perspective."

Eric removed his glasses, folded them, and replaced them in his shirt pocket. He stood silent looked around the room. Jacob believed he saw Eric look into every set of eyes. No one in the room moved. Everyone sat, as if transfixed, as if the entire congregation was holding its breath.

"There is a way that seems right to a man, but the end thereof is death," Eric said at last. "Wide is the gate and broad is the road that leads to destruction, and many enter through it. Today I have set before you life and death, blessings and curses. I implore you, choose life!"

Eric drew in a deep breath, and looked at Jacob. Jacob knew what was coming. He gave him a nod to continue. Eric turned his eyes back to the crowd.

"What kind of pastor would I be if I told you how to find death, but didn't tell you how to find life? The path to life, the narrow path, the one that leads through the through narrow gate; the five-barred gate if you will can only be found in one person—Jesus Christ, the Son of the Living God. You've all heard the most famous verse in the Bible. John 3:16 says:

"For God so loved the world that he gave his one and only Son, that whoever believes in him shall not perish but have eternal life."

"It's true. Why did he die for us, you may ask. Paul tells us in his letter to the Romans, *For all have sinned and fall short of the glory of God*, and then he wrote, *For the wages of sin is death, but the gift of God is eternal life in Christ Jesus our Lord.*

"All means *all*. Every last one of us, from the Pope and the president to the drunk in the gutter and the stripper dancing on a table in a so-called gentlemen's club. We *all* have sinned, therefore we all need a savior.

"But I'm here today to tell you the Good News. *"God demonstrated his love for us in this: While we were still sinners, Christ died for us."* He didn't wait until we got our act together. He didn't wait until we took our Saturday night bath and got all cleaned up and smelling pretty. He sent His Son while we were still in the middle of our sins, in our addictions, in our adulteries, in our hatred and prejudice and greed. It was true 2,000 years ago. It's still true today. God sent His one and *only* Son, that *whosoever*, that means *you-soever*, believes will receive eternal life, eternal joy.

"The path to life is narrow, but it's simple. Believe that Jesus is who He said He is. Admit that you are a sinner, ask Him for forgiveness, then repent. Repenting is an action; it means turning your back on your sin and heading in the opposite direction. Then you will inherit eternal life. Give Him your sins; He gives you life abundantly." Eric smiled again.

"I'm not asking you to commit to some religious rules and regulations. That will just bind you up. I'm not asking you to follow me; I'm a sinful man and at some point I will fail you. I'm not asking you to join this or any congregation. Local congregations are like hospitals, they're full of sick, broken, wounded, dying people who are trying to get better.

"No, I'm inviting you to walk with the only person who was truly worthy to be followed; Jesus Christ. This is your opportunity to stand, walk up to the front, and say, 'Yes Lord! I need you!'"

Jacob held his breath. He remembered his own salvation experience—in that cold cell when he made his decision. He wanted people to share that experience, but he could feel the divided hearts in the room. He felt the needs and desires of every person. He closed his eyes and prayed for courage for all seated with him.

He must have been weeping because he felt a tiny hand on his leg. "Daddy okay?" Jacob took Michael in his arm and hugged him. He felt Renae's hand on his shoulder. He prayed for them, that he would be the man of God he was called to be. That he would be there when the call came upon Michael. That his life would be all the testimony his son needed to choose Christ.

Jacob heard the shuffling of feet, and raised his eyes to the front. At first there were only a few, then others followed, then dozens walked to the front to be prayed for and to give their hearts to Christ. Unashamed tears flowed down Jacob's face as he realized that whatever was to become of Eric, this church, this building, or to him and Renae—it didn't matter. All that did matter were moments like this, when lives were being changed for the Kingdom of God.

As the altar call came to an end, Eric extended his hand over the crowd and offered a blessing in the name of Jesus Christ. "Lord, may we walk from this place changed. May we see the world through Your eyes and not through the eyes of popular opinion. Walk with us down the narrow path and grant us joy, even our darkest hours. Amen."

Frank and the band played a joyous refrain, and people broke into spontaneous laughter, weeping, hugs, and hand-shakes. Eric was focused on a talking with a teen who had come to him directly. The tears in his eyes said it all. The young man had found God. Through the crowd another man walked down the aisle, but not to find Christ. It was Official Edwards, and he had come to claim his prize.

He approached Eric, clapping his hands in mock applause. "Well done, citizen. A marvelous example of trickery from a brilliant con-artist. You had to know this was going to end badly for you. Now, are we going to do this the easy way, or the hard way?" He pulled his club from its holster and held it at his side.

Eric rose to his full height, shoulders back, eyes level. There was no fear, no regret in his gaze, only sorrow for a man so lost in sin that he could see the answer to his heartache and pain. "I have no desire to fight you, Official Edwards. I will come peacefully."

Standing behind Edwards, Jacob saw Jesse, who fixed him with a stare, his eyes pleading, *No!* He shook his head to let him know things were about to get ugly, that Edwards wanted a fight here and now.

Jacob couldn't help himself. He did the one thing he swore an oath not to do. He stood up and placed himself between Eric and Edwards.

"If you're going to get to Eric, you'll have to go through me," Jacob challenged.

"Jacob, don't do this," Eric breathed.

'It's alright, Eric; I know what I'm doing."

"Is that a fact?" Edwards said with a sly grin. He jabbed the butt end of his club into Jacob's gut, causing him to double over. Then swung his club against Jacob's head, knocking him to the ground. Blood gushed from the wound and flowed into his eyes. The last thing he saw was the terrified look on Renae's face. The last thing he heard was Edwards voice whispering, "If you think this is bad, just wait till you wake up, citizen. That's when the real fun begins."

$$\cancel{||||}\ \cancel{||||}\ \cancel{||||}\ \cancel{||||}\ \cancel{||||}\ |||$$

Jacob woke to the sound of a dripping faucet. The darkness that surrounded him hid its location, but every splash was a snare drum beating within his aching head. In attempt to gain some relief, he tried to rub his temple, but his swollen eye only aggravated the pain. Further exploration of his face revealed crusted and dried blood where Edwards had struck him. He remembered the jab to the gut and the head wallop, but how he got here was fuzzy. Unfortunately, he knew where here was.

After trying to lift himself ended with his arms collapsing, Jacob resigned to remaining on the floor. It was cooler there anyhow. It then dawned on him that Eric was arrested as well.

"Eric?" Jacob called out, but his only greeting was silence. He tried to stand again, this time managing to rise to his knees. The room, what he could make of it through his one undamaged eye, was a spinning blur. The methodical drip continued. He finally realized it was coming from inside the room. The puzzle pieces snapped into place. He was in *that* room, the one he heard from his cell in the detention center—the one he dreamed about.

Kenneth came to his mind. He had only been in this room in his dreams. And Kenneth always laid on the floor in a puddle of blood. In a way, he was glad it was dark. *Out of sight, out of mind*, he thought, but he couldn't get Kenneth's fate out of his mind. Or Eric's fate. Or his own fate.

His thoughts turned back to the last moments of the service, and the look on Jesse's face that said it all, that Eric wasn't going to get out in one piece or even alive. He knew he had to do something, that he couldn't just stand by and allow Edwards to take his friend to his death without trying to do anything about it. So he stepped in. *And now here I am again*, he thought. *At least this time I'm in for doing something good.*

The sound of boots thudding down the hallway reverberated off the walls, growing louder until they stopped just outside the door. Keys jingled followed by the click of the lock. A bright light blinded his good eye as the door squealed open. "About time you woke up, citizen. On your feet. Official Edwards wants to see you."

"Where am I?"

"Back where you belong. Stupid stunt. But the result is, now we have two trophies instead of one."

"Shut up, Anderson. Just bring him."

Anderson grabbed Jacob by the arm and pulled him to his feet and out into the hallway. As his good eye began to adjust to the sudden brightness, he could make out doors lining the walls. *Just like in my dreams.* They turned a corner, climbed a small flight of stairs, and stopped in front of another cell door. Jacob was breathing hard from the exertion, and every heartbeat pounded in his ears. Anderson unlocked the cell door, opened it, and shoved Jacob through. He fell over something and collapsed on the floor.

"We'll be back for the two of you shortly," Turner said, his voice flat, emotionless.

Jacob rolled onto his back and tried to regain his breath and his equilibrium. *What did I stumble over? Wait, did he say the two of you?* With his eye adjusted again to the dim light he saw a pair of feet. *Oh, no.*

"Eric?"

"You gave me your word you would do nothing," Eric gently chided as he helped Jacob to sit.

"I had to do something," Jacob defended himself. "The look on Jesse's face said it was going to be much worse that you or I expected. I couldn't stand by and do nothing. I wouldn't have been able to live with myself."

"What about Renae and Michael?"

"I don't think they could have lived with myself either," Jacob attempted a poor joke. "I think Renae will understand. Not doing something would have been worse."

Eric nodded. "For what it's worth, Thank you. But I'm not sure either of us will get out of this alive."

"You're welcome," Jacob said. "And for what it's worth, we've always been in God's hands. If the time is now, so be it."

Eric looked at Jacob, then the door, then tapped his ear and pointed to the ceiling. Jacob remembered, *'The walls have ears.'*

"Bottom line," Jacob said. "If I hadn't been put in this place in the first place, I would have never met you. If I had never met you, I would have never met Jesus. I heard a wise man say that joy was about perspective. Edwards did me a favor by putting me in..." Jacob paused, and pointed. "Well, would you look at that?"

Etched with precision into the wall were 18 five-barred gates. They were in Jacob's old cell. "Looks like I've come full circle," Jacob smiled.

The door rattled, then opened. A billow of cigar smoke wafted in, followed by the familiar figure of Official Edwards. "Well, well, well," he hissed. "Seems we have all come full circle, gentlemen. And I'm not fond of circles. The question is what do we do about it? You spread your propaganda and offend people. I tell you to stop. You do it anyway. You get arrested and spend a little time as guests of the state. I let you out with a stern warning not to do it again. But what do you do? You deliberately disobey my orders, and here you are again.

"Your lack of respect is bad to my jurisdiction. People see one citizen taking the law into his own hands, and it causes others with the same delusions to raise their voices. Then it's nothing but work, work, work for me. Is that what you want? Is this some kind of personal vendetta against me? Honestly, if that's all it was, I could look the other way. But I think you want to start a revolution. And I just can't let that happen; not on my watch."

Edwards took a deep drag of his cigar, then blew the smoke in Eric's face.

"Now, here's what I don't understand. You knew we were watching you. We did everything we could to put the fear of god—well, the fear of me—into you. Even went so far as to burn down your friend's old barn—"

"You went so far as to commit murder," Eric said flatly.

"That was an accident," Edwards declared. "We didn't know the guy was still inside. It was late. We thought he was already at his home in bed. Still, it sent a pretty strong message, wouldn't you say? I was sure that would encourage your little band of believers to disband. But nothing I did seemed to have any effect, other than pouring gasoline on a fire. Now, I have to tell you gentlemen, you are stepping on my last nerve. And it's got to stop. So here's the real question, Mr. Anderson," he addressed Jacob. "What's it going to take?

Am I going to have to go after your wife and child too, like I did with Lassiter's family?"

The reality of the situation crashed in on Jacob. *Edwards had killed Eric's family. Would he actually kill Renae and Michael?* Jacob studied the Officials face, and realized the man was capable of any atrocity. Jacob closed his eyes, took a breath, prayed for guidance, and made a decision. "You know Official Edwards, I used to be afraid of you. There was a time when just the whiff of your cigar smoke gave me the shivers. But now? Not so much. You think by killing me, killing my family, you silence us? We won't be the first to die for our faith, and we certainly won't be the last. The funny thing is, I do not hate you. I feel sorry for you."

"You. Feel sorry for me? Huh." Edwards pondered for a moment, then drew his silver pistol from its new leather holster and fired a single shot into Eric's chest.

$$\cancel{||||}\ \cancel{||||}\ \cancel{||||}\ \cancel{||||}\ \cancel{||||}\ ||||$$

"Eric!" Jacob screamed.

Eric fell to his knees, clutching his chest. He looked down at his wound, then up to Jacob.

Jacob knelt beside Eric and gathered his friend in his arms. He pressed his hand against the wound, trying to staunch the flow of blood. "I'm sorry, Eric. I'm so sorry. This is my fault," he wept.

Eric grasped his hand and managed to gasp, "God's plan Jake, God's plan. My gate has closed, but yours is just opening. Walk through. Don't be afraid. Don't be afraid. Fear… not." Eric wheezed and coughed, then did not breath again.

Quick footsteps pounded down the hall. Jesse appeared in the doorway to the cell. "I heard gunshots. What happened?" he demanded.

"Not your concern Jesse," Edwards said. "Go back to what you were doing. We need those witness statements in detail."

Jesse surveyed the scene, his eyes darting from the dead man to the gun in Edwards' hand. "Edwards, what did you do?"

"You forget yourself, Durrant. It's Official Edwards to you."

"You can't just shoot an unarmed man, Edwards."

"I'm an Official. I can do anything I damn well please. Who do you think you are to question what I can or can't do? I'll have your badge. I'll throw you so far into the darkest level of these cells you'll never see the light of day again. So, Deputy Official Durrant, choose you this day who you will serve. Are you going to go back upstairs and do your job, or do you disappear? Your choice. There are plenty of other applicants dying to have your position."

Jesse's cheek twitched as his jaw clenched. But he said, "Yes, sir," then turned on his heel an strode away.

"You're a bastard Edwards," Jacob said between heartbroken sobs. "Only a coward would shoot an unarmed man."

"Bastard, yes," Edwards admitted. "But coward? No, I wouldn't say that. A coward accepts whatever fate throws at him. I depend on myself, not some mythical supreme being. I am the captain of my fate. I choose my own destiny. You, on the other hand, are the real coward. Your friend is dying in your arms, a victim of the actions of another mortal man. And what is your god doing to save him? Nothing. Perhaps if your god actually existed, he would have caused that bullet to bounce off his chest, or go right through him without causing any damage at all. Or maybe your god will bring Mr. Lassiter back to life. If he did that, I might actually believe. But Mr. Lassiter is dead. I took his life. Who's the god now, Mr. Andrews?"

Jacob laid the empty shell that once contained Eric's soul on the cell floor, and stood glaring at Edwards.

Edwards had seen that look in the eyes of more criminals than he cared to remember. It was the dictionary definition of, *If looks could kill*. He raised his revolver and aimed it at Jacob. "Relax citizen. This bullet is not meant for you. I have no desire to kill you. You are going to be my witness to the uttermost parts of the world. Come along while I explain it to you." He motioned toward the cell door with his gun.

Jacob gave one last look, took a cleansing breath, and stumbled into the hall and up the stairs toward Edwards' office. He sat down in the room where they had their first meeting. His gaze took in the Official's private arsenal, neatly arranged on shelves of the wall, it seems a bit larger than he remembered.

"Yes, I've added to my collection," Edwards boasted, noticing Jacob's reaction. He sat down at his desk, placed his cigar in an ashtray, and spoke to Jacob like they were two college buddies catching up. "A couple more guns, a few more grenades from different eras and countries. You'd be amazed at how the construction varies from country to country. Don't you touch them, though. Some of those are still live. But let's cut to the chase, Mr. Andrews. One man dies in custody, trying to wrestle a firearm from an official, well, people tend to look the other way. But two prisoners dying on the same day? Well, that's just bad form. And I have to conjure up another excuse to explain both of your deaths, and that's just a lot of work.

"Now it's time for us to work together to undo all this unpleasantness and get back to normal. What do you say? Wanna play ball, Mr. Andrews?"

"I don't play ball with pond scum," Jacob spat. "Besides, why would you possibly trust me? What makes you think I won't go public the first chance I get?"

"Two reasons," Edwards laughed, enjoying the repartee. "One—your lovely wife. Two—your precious little boy. You wouldn't want to see then suffer the same fate as Mr. Lassiter's family, now would you?"

"You mean to say you killed—"

"I mean to say nothing, Mr. Andrews. But it is true that

there are some very careless drivers out there. It's such a shame, too. Lassiter's wife and daughters were lovely, and by all accounts very pleasant people." Edwards paused to take another drag on his cigar.

"Yes, Mr. Lassiter was a strong-willed man, one that could not be broken. And I should know. I tried, and I'm very good at my job. But you, citizen? I know you. You're not half the man Lassiter was. I believe you value your wife and child far more than you value your new-found faith. You know I could take your son's life with the snap of my fingers. I don't believe that is a price you are willing to pay. So, yes, I feel comfortable letting you go back to your little life, with your little wife and your little boy. And all you have to do is agree to knock off this nonsense about a non-existent god.

"It's not that hard to imagine, Mr. Andrews. You were in trying circumstances. You were duped by a great con artist. Once you were on the inside, it was like a drug. You were hooked. You needed that high. But you can overdose on a drug, Mr. Andrews. So, we've help to wean you off Lassiter's influence. You've returned to your senses, and you've lost your desire for it. And when you tell the deluded masses of your recovery, *they* will lose the desire for it, and as our dear departed friend so aptly put it this morning, they will simply disappear back into the herd."

Edwards clamped his teeth around his cigar and talk around the stogie. "Have I made your position clear, citizen?"

"Crystal," Jacob seethed. "I shut up, or you hurt my family."

"See, that wasn't so hard. I knew you were a man who could be reasoned with."

"I'm not sure my cooperation will do you much good though," Jacob said. "You didn't just silence a voice of opposition. You made Eric Lassiter into a martyr. A man who died for the faith is a powerful symbol. Strike the shepherd and the sheep will scatter. That is true. But they will come together again. They will rise up, and there is nothing you or anyone else can do about it. There are more of us than you could possibly believe."

"My dear citizen," Edwards grin was cold, vindictive, evil. "That's where you come in. It's the only reason you are still alive. Regardless of their number, your job is to convince Lassiter's former followers to disband. You will reinforce the fear. You will instigate their paranoia. You will remove every thought about making any kind of stand."

"I can't do that."

"Can't or won't?"

"Both. Either. Take your pick."

"I'll be sure and tell Renae your response next time I see her."

"Edwards, I'm just a man. Nothing I say to anyone can snuff out their personal experiences with a Holy God. They'll see right through it. They would know I was lying to protect my family."

Edwards rubbed the bridge of his nose, as if to fight off an impending headache. "I had hoped it wouldn't come to this, but it appears you leave me know choice. Mr. Andrews, I'm sure you knew I was sending in undercover agents to serve as witnesses. Perhaps you didn't know that they weren't there to observe Mr. Lassiter. They were there to observe you. And you played right into my hands."

Jacob shot him a confused glance, which caused Edwards to chuckle with glee.

"Much like you, we had a traitor in our midst," Edwards confided in a low voice. But unlike you, I know who our betrayer was. That's right, Mr. Andrews. Our betrayer was your friend Jesse. I let him know that Mr. Lassiter was not going to leave that church alive. I knew he would tip you off. He did, as I knew he would. And you stood your ground, as I knew you would. And I have a room full of witnesses that saw it. I have plenty of evidence to put you away until you are a very, *very* old man.

There was a sharp knock on the door followed by Jesse sticking his head in and waving Edwards over. Jacob could make out the conversation but it sounded like several of the witnesses were recanting their testimony.

Edwards burst back into the room, grumbling to himself. He pulled out his baton and slapped against his palm.

"Bad news?" Jacob asked, trying to suppress a grin.

Edwards raised his club as if to bludgeon Jacob with it, then thought better of it. He tossed the baton onto his desk and laughed. "Temporary setback, perhaps. Nothing that cannot be dealt with. But now, back to our arrangement. So, tell me—shall I send a car to retrieve your wife and child?"

From somewhere inside, Jacob experienced a peace he didn't realize was possible. Words flooded his mind. *God is in control. Even when things are at their darkest, that fact never changes. God is in control.* Jacob wobbled on his feet, the adrenaline rush wearing off and his injuries once again asserting themselves.

"I'm sorry, Mr. Edwards," Jacob said, doing his best to remain upright. "But I'm just not afraid of you, or any of your threats anymore. For me to live is Christ, and to die is gain. Kill me; kill them—we don't grieve like those who have no hope. We will be re-united. You may have killed Eric's body, but his spirit is alive and unbound. He did the job that was destined for him here on earth. I'll do the job God had destined for me. Do what you have to do. I will not be silenced." Jacob paused for a moment, then a smile creased his face and he added, "If something needs saying, I'll say it!"

Edwards drew his revolver and fired, nicking Jacob's left should. "I am an expert marksman," Edwards said coldly. "I assure you, that was not a miss; just an attention getter. I suggest you reconsider."

Jacob stared at the instrument of his impending death. He wished he could have had one more moment with Renae, to tell her he loved her, to tell her to stand firm, to tell her goodbye.

"Not a chance in hell," he declared. He closed his eyes and waited for the inevitable.

"As you wish, citizen," Edwards took his time cocking the revolver and drawing a bead between Jacob's eyes. Jesse appears in the doorway as Edwards started to squeeze the trigger.

"No!" he shouted and flung himself between Edwards and Jacob.

Edwards stared at the dead man on the floor of his office and shook his head in disgust. "Traitor," he muttered under his breath. He took a couple of steps forward toward Jacob. "See all the trouble you've caused. Because of your stubbornness, two men are dead. Of course this traitor would have had to be eliminated anyway, but there are cleaner ways of handling it. No matter. What's done is done."

Edwards strolled back to his chair and sat. Jacob could almost see the wheels turning inside Edwards' head; plotting his next move. He was taken back, but still kept his revolver trained on Jacob. Then he smiled. "Two bodies would raise questions, but three?" He took a drag of his cigar and blew it out, "Heh, it's cut and dry."

Edwards stood and looked down at Jesse. "Such a pity," he said. "A good man like Deputy Durrant, tried to restrain a violent prisoner, when that prisoner managed to get hold of the deputy's side arm and kill him. How does it feel, Mr. Andrews, being tagged a murderer. Yes, Jesse Durrant was a hero. He killed Mr. Lassiter as he was trying to escape, and you killed Jesse for killing your friend. Then I killed you for murdering an Official in cold blood. All wrapped in a perfect little bow. Absolutely perfect!"

Jacob was shocked the rapidity of Edwards' descent into madness. The Official pounded on his desk, waving his weapon at Jacob, pointing first at his head, then at his legs, then at his check. He laughed. He took another drag on his cigar. And he completely failed to see Jesse regain his feet and move behind him.

Jesse's radio on his belt screeched. It was Anderson "Jesse, what's going on in there? We heard shots fired." Edwards spun around in time to see Jesse ready to pounce. He fired a wild shot, catching him in the shoulder and knocking him back against the wall of weapons.

Jesse leaned against it for a moment, before turning toward Jacob. "Forgive me. Tell Renae I am sorry. Now—run!"

Jacob saw a grenade in Jesse's good hand. Jesse raised it to his mouth and pulled the pin with his teeth. "Get out of here, Jacob," he screamed and charged at Edwards. Edwards emptied his revolver into Jesse's chest, but the younger man's momentum carried him forward. He was already dead when he collided with Edwards, knocking him into of his chair then onto the floor.

Jacob tumbled out of the open door and pulled himself into a protective crouch as all hell broke loose inside the office. Flames, smoke, and debris swirled around him. Smoke detectors squealed, and the automatic sprinkler system rained down showering everything in water.

Jacob's ear rang. He was disoriented and in shock, but he knew he needed to be somewhere else when the authorities arrived. He stumbled toward an illuminated EXIT sign, and wandered past a desk with a set of keys marked GMC. He snatched them up and limped through the exit. There were two Denalis in the parking lot. He pushed the unlock button, and Jesse's chirped. He climbed in, pushed the start button and slammed it into reverse. "The Party's Over" blaring out of the speakers. He turned the stereo off, popped it into drive and sped out of the parking lot. Once a couple of blocks away he slowed down—*No reason to attract attention*, he reasoned. Two fire department vehicles passed him, moving in the opposite direction with their sirens screaming. He assumed they were heading toward the precinct.

Still in shock, Jacob was confused, weak, unsure of where to go or even where he was. He drove down the highway until he didn't see another vehicle, then pulled off onto a dirt road that led into a tree line. He maneuvered the truck behind a copse of trees, turned the engine off, leaned his head back and just breathed. He still couldn't see out of one eye, but at least the ringing in his ears had subsided. *What just happened?* He pondered. *Is it really over, or just beginning? Edwards is gone. And Jesse… Jesse sacrificed his life to save me.*

He shook his head, willing his confused thoughts to take shape. The only thing that was clear at that moment was Renae and Michael. He needed to reach them. Then he need to rest, to clear his thoughts. He leaned back in the seat and raised his face to the heavens, praying for guidance. When he opened his eyes, he saw a little blue button with a star above the word, "On." "Thank you Lord," he breathed. "And thank you Jesse." He pushed the button.

"On-star, how can we help you, Jesse?"

"Call Renae," Jacob said.

"Thank you, Jesse. Your call is being placed."

The phone rang several times. *Com'on, com'on, com'on*, he mentally urged her, realizing Renae might see Jesse's name on her caller ID and not answer.

"Hello?"

"Renae, it's Jacob."

"Jacob? What happened to you? Why are you calling from—"

"No time to explain. Are you and Michael alright?"

"Yes, we are fine. We're up at my parents. Jacob, I don't under—"

"I will tell you everything when I get there. Just trust me. I'll see you soon," Jacob said. "Renae, I love you."

"I love you too. See you soon."

Jacob started the truck and pointed it back toward the highway. Between the copse and the road was a gate. A five-barred gate. It stood open. He had seen that gate before, perhaps in a dream. Jacob smiled. He was on the right path.

$\text{IIII IIII IIII IIII IIII IIII}$

The highways were clear, and being in an Officials vehicle ensured no law enforcement officer would stop him. At least not until they figured out the debacle at the precinct. He hoped Renae wouldn't be frightened when he arrived in Jesse's truck, but he didn't want to say anything over the phone. If he had learned anything in the past few months, it was that private conversations were no longer private.

Jacob pulled off the country road and into the driveway that led up to the stately, old-fashioned southern home that belonged to Renae's parent. Two stories, white with green shutters, and a wrap-around porch, it was the epitome of southern grace and charm. Renae was sitting in a rocking chair next to a side door when he pulled up. When she saw him emerge from Jesse's truck, she rushed down the steps and into his arms, tears streaming down her face.

"Jacob, I thought you were dead for real this time." She took a moment to look at him and started weeping again. "You're covered in blood. Where are you hurt? What's going on?"

Jacob managed a weak smile, held up a hand to stop her questions, and said, "Could we maybe sit down? Then I'll tell you everything."

Renae let him lean on her as he limped onto the porch where he collapsed onto the rocking chair Renae had previously occupied. "It's all over the news," Renae said through her tears. There was some sort of explosion at the precinct in Carrelton. Three people are dead. But that's all they are saying. I thought one of them was you." She burst out crying again.

"Babe, I am okay. Better than okay now that I'm with you. Trust me, I look worse than I feel. But the news is far from good. Sit down and I'll give you the short version."

Still trembling, she took several deep breaths and managed to stop weeping. "Okay," she said, "so tell me."

"I'll start with the end and work backward. I will explain everything, but it might take a while so please, just bear with me," Jacob began. He looked Renae in the eye for understanding.

Renae nodded, preparing herself for the worst. "I'm ready."

"Eric, Jesse, and Edwards are all dead."

"What? How? What was the—"

Jacob cut her off. "I'll get to that. I will. Just let me tell the story, then if you have any questions I'll do my best to answer them." He started from the beginning from when he woke up in the cell. He told her of Edwards' threats, about how he killed Eric. "I may have made things worse by telling him we were not afraid to die."

"You challenged him?" Renae asked.

Jacob thought about it for a moment. Not sure if his answer would upset her or make her proud. "Yes, I guess you can say that I did. I wanted to show him that regardless of what happened, he would not win."

"Good for you," she said. "He needed to know God was bigger than any of this. Then what happened?"

"Then he shot at me," Jacob said.

"What? Where?"

Jacob stopped her. "I'm sorry. That came out wrong. He

shot at me, and the bullet grazed my shoulder. He said he missed on purpose, but the next one wouldn't. That's when…" Jacob choked back his own tears as the event of those next few moments played again in his memory.

Renae took his hand. "Go on."

"Jesse stepped in, Renae. He took the bullet for me. Edwards thought he was dead. So did I. I can't explain it, but Edwards seemed to totally lose control. He was talking to himself, waving his gun around, laughing. It was surreal. But Jesse wasn't dead. Neither of us noticed when he got up. I can still hear him yelling for me to get away and leave right before he pulled the pin on that grenade."

Renae was sobbing into Jacob's shoulder now. He soothed her as best he could.

"There is one other thing," Jacob said, tilting her head up to look into her eyes. "He said to tell you he was sorry."

"Deep inside, he was a good man? You know that, right, Jacob?"

"Yes, I know."

"No, I mean it. He never laid a hand on me," she explained. "I think it's important you know that. He respected me and Michael in every way."

"Thank you for telling me that," Jacob said. "He told me the same thing the other night. I guess I always knew, but your confirmation means a lot."

The notification tone on Renae's phone went off. She grabbed it. It was for a local news story. She clicked on it, and it took her to a story:

AP - Three men are dead at Carrelton Precinct Number 2. Their bodies were found on location after an explosion ripped through the building earlier today. One man, 28-year-old, Jacob Andrews, is being sought for questioning regarding the matter.

"They're looking for you, Jake."

"I figured it was only a matter of time," Jacob said. He read the story off her phone, "When they realize that Jesse's truck is gone, it won't take them long to put two and two together. They'll run the GPS. That will lead them here. I need to go back."

"What? Why? Who are you going to talk to who will give you the benefit of the doubt?"

"I don't know yet. Maybe one of the local police captains. They were usually against other agencies treading on their jurisdiction. Frank knows the Captain of the Polk Police Department. Maybe he can put me get in touch with him. Either way, I have to turn myself in. I won't be a fugitive. I won't subject you and Michael to being the family of a fugitive." Jacob gathered himself and stood. He kissed Renae on the forehead. "I love you, babe, don't worry. Everything will be okay. God is in control."

"I know, but that doesn't stop me from being concerned." She reached out to hug him, resulting in a grimace of pain.

"Plus, I really need to see a doctor. At least in custody, I'll get medical attention."

"Be careful," Renae said. "I love you, too."

"I will," Jacob walks down the steps. "Give love to Michael for me. Tell him I will see him soon."

Jacob climbed back in the borrowed vehicle and started back toward town. He used the On-star to call Frank. "You sure he can be trusted, Frank?" Jacob asked.

"We go way back, Jacob. He's as good as they come."

"Your approval is good enough for me," Jacob said. "Tell him I'm about 30 minutes out, and I'm unarmed. Tell him to be ready."

Jacob arrived at the Polk Police Department shortly after 6:00 p.m. The sun was on the horizon and heading down. A tall gentleman dressed in blue from head to toe, stood at the end of the walkway, waiting. His salt and pepper hair flowed seamlessly into his beard. Jacob parked and approached him. "Are you Jacob Andrews?"

"Yes, sir." Jacob was nervous. He wasn't sure if this man was a friend or foe. "Yes, I am. I am here to surrender myself and to answer questions about this morning's events in Carrelton."

Jacob extended his arms, wrists close together. Hoffman said, "There will be no need for cuffs. Frank Dunham has vouched for you. His word is good enough for me. Walk this way please."

Jacob followed Captain Hoffman into the station. They were quickly buzzed through the entrance when he gave the woman behind a plexiglass partition a hand motion. Hoffman led him down a hall and into an office with Captain D. Hoffman on the door in bold black letter.

"Please, have a seat, Mr. Andrews."

Jacob had had his fill of law enforcement offices and was feeling a little jittery. Hoffman picked up on it. "Jacob, there is no need to worry. I have been authorized to ask you a few questions. There will be no Federal Officials here. At least not if I have anything to say about it. You are safe here."

"I have seen enough these past few months to last me a lifetime. I don't know who to trust anymore."

"Maybe this will help," Hoffman reached into his inner breast pocket. He pulled out a folded item. He handed it to Jacob. Jacob smiled and was relieved in an instant when he saw it was a bulletin from the service. "I am on your side, Jacob. Like Will told you, there are more of us than you know. People who you know you can trust when things go to pot."

"I am relieved," Jacob said.

"You been listening to any of the recent news reports?" Hoffman asked.

"No," Jacob said. "I've been doing my best to just avoid any undue attention."

"Then you haven't heard?" Hoffman asked.

"Heard what?"

"You have been exonerated. Yes, we have some questions, but not in the way you may think. We are not seeking you because you're a suspect. They are seeking you now because you are a prime witness."

Jacob's eyes widened.

"Here, let me show you," Hoffman pulled up an email attachment on his computer. As he was doing so, Jacob noticed something on his desk. He had a couple of his Captain pins sitting on the desk. They were side by side. Up against each other, they resembled a five-barred gate. Jacob knew he was in the right place.

"Here it is." Hoffman turned the computer toward Jacob. "Just click on the play button."

A buffering screen finally reached 100 and Jesse's face appeared on the screen. He was looking to his left, then to the camera. "I don't know how much time I have left. I am Jesse Durrant, a Lieutenant in Carrelton, Texas under Official Nathan Edwards. I am making this video to let everyone know the truth about what happened here today."

Jacob looked up at Hoffman, confused. Hoffman pointed at the screen, "It gets better. Keep watching."

"I first want to say that Jacob Andrews is innocent of any

charges that have been brought up against him. He was being used by this office to find fault in a man named Eric Lassiter. Lassiter was a local minister who yesterday held a service that was interpreted as a violation of the new federal Anti-Dehumanization Act. About 10 minutes ago, Reverend Eric Lassiter was gunned down in cold blood by Captain Nathan Edwards. Reverend Lassiter was unarmed and in a federal prison cell when he was murdered."

"Captain Edwards has been chasing Lassiter across the country because of the case they both were involved in back in Atlanta several years ago. Once here, he found Lassiter and had him arrested. After a year of imprisonment, he was released, and we were tasked with observing him until he broke the law again.

"When he finally did, we took Lassiter into custody as well as Jacob Andrews, one of Lassiter's trusted followers. It was during the processing procedures that Captain Edwards shot and killed Lassiter. After murdering Lassiter, he told me that he was going to make one final attempt to stop Mr. Andrews by threatening his wife and their three-year-old son."

Jesse ran his hands down his face and shook his head, "I can no longer continue in this position knowing how many people are being hurt by this lunatic. I don't know how this will end. Should I die, I want those watching this to know that Jacob Andrews is innocent of any accusations. I need to go now. Go and save the day. Goodbye." The video ended with the replay icon on the screen.

"This was sent to an anonymous source who got it to a local news station. As you can see, Lieutenant Durrant has completely exonerated you." Hoffman turned the computer back toward him. "Now I just need a statement from you as to what happened after that video was made."

Jacob explained everything. From the fire at Will's shop to Jesse using the grenade that caused the explosion. He explained why he felt the need to flee, and why he returned when he heard on the news that they were searching for him.

Hoffman recorded Jacob's statement. "That's some story," he declared. "It jives with what preliminary forensics are showing."

"One more thing, Captain. I came back to clear my name, and because it was the right thing to do. But I also came back because of the two remaining deputies under Edwards."

"Funny you should mention them." Hoffman pulled out a file from the bottom of stack of identical folders, and tossed it on the desk in front of Jacob. "That fire up in New Braunfels you mentioned, the one where your friend died."

"Will Johnson," Jacob said, opening the folder. It was the report on the fire at Will's shop.

"The regular county arson investigator was out of the country on vacation when that happened. Our investigator took his place on that case. His findings were inconclusive, so the fire was deemed an accident, but it still looked suspicious. There were fragments the scientist could not identify. Until today," Hoffman explained.

"CSI found similar pieces of shrapnel at the precinct."

"Edwards collected weapons, including live explosive devices," Jacob confirmed. "He loved showing them off."

"Now if our scientist had not been up in New B for that investigation, this connection wouldn't have been made. When we questioned those two gentlemen about them, they appeared to be more nervous than one might expect. Well, let's just say one thing led to another and the end result is those two are now in county lock-up awaiting the forensic results of certain materials found in their possession. Now, it looks to me like you could use some medical attention. We're gonna have to keep the Denali, but I'll have one of my officers drive you over to Regional Medical Center to get you patched up."

Jacob bowed his head, his energy spent. "So, that's it? I'm free?"

Hoffman grinned. "Far as we're concerned. Unless you got something else you want to confess to."

"No. No, sir. It's just that—That's amazing. I don't believe it."

Hoffman pressed a button on his intercom and said, "Sharon, would you send Officer Pate to my office. I have a gentlemen who needs a ride to the hospital."

Jacob sat back in his chair pondering the turn of events. He felt liberated. No more hiding. No more secret meetings. Eric had accomplished what he set out to do, though it cost him his life. He fulfilled his calling, even though he was not about to pass through the closed five-barred gate. Now it was Jacob turn to pick up the mantle Eric had left behind. He was ready to walk through his own gate; ready to face whatever was on the other side.

One month later…

"Do you remember what you are going to say?" Renae said she straightened Jacob's tie.

"Yes, I remember," Jacob insisted. "I've been practicing for almost a week now. Still, I have to confess, I'm a little nervous. I've never spoken in front of this many people before."

"For all things there is a first time," Renae quoted.

"Is that from Ecclesiastes? King Solomon?

"Wrath of Khan. Mr. Spock," Renae giggled.

"Well, at least it wasn't from the book of Hezekiah," Jacob chuckled. "Eric really got me with that one."

"You'll do fine love. Just let God lead you. And don't let up."

"Of course not," Jacob laughed. "When have you seen me let up?"

The converted choir room was once again filled with people. They managed to squeeze a few more chairs in this time, but the room was packed wall to wall—with many standing in the back, all to pay their respects to the deceased.

Jacob walked up to the podium still in front of the five five-barred gates. Two easels held large poster board photos on either side of the podium, floral wreaths were situated on either side of those. Jacob took the mic and flipped the switch on, causing a loud pop from the speakers. Billy Jr. waived his hand in the air in apology.

"Can everyone hear me?" Jacob began. "Good. I have the

honor of delivering a eulogy for our two fallen friends. To my left you see Jesse. Many of you, perhaps most of you, didn't know Jesse, but he and I go way back. He was my best friend. Then he wasn't, mostly because I was foolish, and stupid, and took for granted everything and everyone around me. Then, by a miracle of God, my life was changed. And because of that miracle, our friendship was reconciled. In his final moments, before he sacrificed his life for me, we made amends. The Lord Jesus Himself declared that no man had greater love than this, that he lay down his life for his friend. Jesse was my friend.

"The miracle I spoke of was possible because of the man you see pictured on my right, Pastor Eric Lassiter. For if it weren't for him I would still be stuck in the same self-destructive habits that landed me in prison in the first place."

"Jesse and Eric could not have been more different. Yet these two men both displayed extraordinary acts of courage—extraordinary acts of love. Both faced with a life and death decision. They chose life for you and for me, and it cost them their lives in this world. I am a blessed man to have been able to call these men my brothers.

"Each of us has our own story to tell, of how we were drawn into a deeper relationship with Christ because of one man's passion for the Gospel, the Good News. If something needed saying, he said it. Even when it cost him everything. I think the best way to honor Eric's memory is to simply live to your fullest potential. Stand when no one else will. And realize you are not alone. There are more of us than you know.

"I want to thank everyone for giving me the opportunity to speak about these brothers. I wish they were both here now to join in this ceremony honoring their lives. But the truth is, I don't think they would want to be anywhere else than where they are at this moment—in the presence of God. Any party we could throw here on earth pales in comparison. To God be the glory!"

Amidst the natural sorrow that accompanied death, there was a joyous spirit of celebration that ignited the entire community—that indescribable sense of the Holy Spirit empowering His people permeated the atmosphere. Jacob left the platform to seek out Renae and Michael, then stopped, and returned to the microphone once again.

"Brothers and sisters, tonight we have kept the rocks silent because the joy of the Lord is filling this place. If you were here a month or so ago you heard Pastor Eric's final sermon. But that sermon was not the final word. We are continuing the work the Lord placed in our hands this Sunday. Service starts at 9:00 a.m. and we would love to see you here."

A round of applause erupted. Jacob basked in the warm glow of the infilling work of the Holy Spirit. He couldn't remember feeling so free. He looked up to see Renae beaming, glowing with an inner peace he had not seen before. She pointed at her abdomen, and smiled. Realization crashed in on him, and he grinned from ear to ear as she nodded.

Life was exploding all around him. The life that could only come from God. He recalled Eric's words about walking through that five-barred gate toward his destiny in Christ. He hadn't though he had the strength to move forward without his friend. Now he knew, he had all the support he needed. The power that flowed through Eric, that gave him the courage to face his own closed gate, was alive and flowing through him.

He smiled at his wife, the mother of his children, and took his first step through the opened five-barred gate.

Acknowledgements

The Five Barred Gate began in 2016 as a dream where it was illegal to be a Christian. The concept stood with me for half a year before I did anything with it. Many people went into this novel's formation and eventual final product. I want to take a moment to mention a few.

Jeremy White, the man with the gift of encouragement. You gave me the boost that began this journey. Without our vow to hold each other accountable in our dreams, I never would have put pen to paper to write this novel. I know you don't like the spotlight, but I could not leave you out of this.

Maurice Draine, thank you for taking a chance on the guy who did not want to do research. Through working with you, I learned a great deal about the writing process, and most importantly, the editing process. You helped me believe that I could write anything and gave me the ability to do just that.

Bonniejean Alford, another one of my writing accountability partners. Without your consistent voice in my ear to keep writing, I would not have completed this project. It was your inspiration that enabled me to get that final edit done.

Steve Guidetti, thank you for giving me my first taste of success. "Elissa the Curious Snail," was just something I wrote for my daughter, Audrey, to provide me with some rest from editing this novel. I never knew that a small children's book would give me the courage to take the next step of pursuing a novel.

Sara Harris, thank you for introducing me to Mike and WordCrafts Press. Without your 'good word' and witnessing your success, I would not be where I am today.

Pastor Duane Mayberry, Eric Lassiter is modeled after you. Every word, every inspiration, the attitude toward God and life, all come from the near decade that I have sat under your pastoring First Baptist Church Charlotte. I am sure as our church reads this novel; they too will see you in Eric. Thank you for giving to the Lord; I am a life that was changed. We are all glad that you gave.

Finally, I want to thank the woman behind the curtain, my amazing wife, Carolyn. Thank you for enduring those long nights of me 'Kermitting' away, listening to the constant back and forth about a character or plot holes, and the constant encouragement that I was good enough. You bless me beyond words. I love you and am happy to share this road with you.

Most importantly, thank you, Heavenly Father, for allowing this dream to become a reality. It is all you. I cannot take credit for any of it. Without your direction these words would be useless. Please allow this work to minister to those who read it. Use it to empower a new generation of believers. Allow them to see that there are more of us than they could possibly believe.

Lastly, thank you, dear reader, for giving your time to read this book. It means a lot that you trusted me to entertain, and hopefully excite, you with this story. If you enjoyed this story, would you consider leaving a review wherever you bought this book, or on your favorite social media platform? I want as many readers as possible to discover this story, and your voice can help do that. Leave a review and tell a friend! Word-of-mouth is the best way to introduce this story to other readers.

In His Exciting Service,
Jeff S. Bray

ABOUT THE AUTHOR

Jeff Bray lives in a small town in South Central Texas with his wife Carolyn and their four children. They are members of the local First Baptist Church, serving in a variety of capacities, including teaching Sunday school, working with men's ministry, and managing the church's online presence.

Jeff's passion for writing began in elementary school with a short story about a lost kitten. His circuitous literary career started with his personal blog, Moments for the Heart, which led to small paid assignments before expanding into magazine articles in national publications.

Jeff is the author of the *Elissa the Curious Snail* series of whimsical children's picture books which help parents introduce basic faith concepts like prayer, even in the face of adversity, into their teachings in a fun and entertaining way.

The Five Barred Gate is his first novel.

Connect with Jeff online at: jeffsbrayauthor.com

www.ingramcontent.com/pod-product-compliance
Lightning Source LLC
Chambersburg PA
CBHW050509190726
48284CB00003B/742